ARMY OF THE NIGHT

Something is coming.

I consider turning the headlights of the p-car on and shining them down the road, but I think better of drawing attention to myself. A whistle, a rustle, garb shifting around dusty ankles and legs, and it goes to the core of my white fear in the heart of blackness. Chanting, eerie echoes off blasted walls ravaged by fire, words unexplained. I can see them, perhaps twenty men and women, heads bowed, shuffling through the street, moving toward the old people's compound. A slight sigh of dry wind pushes the white rags marking their area.

I can make out individuals now. Eyes fixed in their heads, they do not blink. Legs moving in unison, they do not deviate. As they turn into the old people's compound, a young girl runs away from their march screaming.

Against all will I move closer.

Books by Eric James Fullilove

CIRCLE OF ONE
THE STRANGER

THE STRANGER

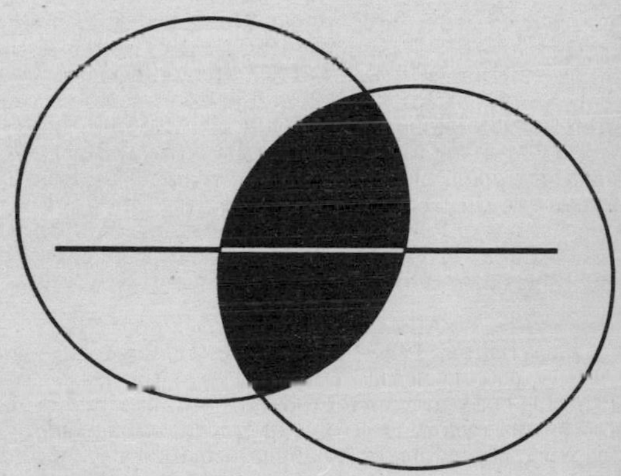

ERIC JAMES FULLILOVE

BANTAM BOOKS

NEW YORK • TORONTO • LONDON • SYDNEY • AUCKLAND

THE STRANGER
A Bantam Spectra Book / November 1997

SPECTRA and the portrayal of a boxed "s" are trademarks of Bantam Books,
a division of Bantam Doubleday Dell Publishing Group, Inc.

Grateful acknowledgment is made for permission to reprint the following: Quote by Satish Kumar and "The Bridge of Well-Being" by Mark Nepo are reprinted from *Parabola: The Magazine of Myth and Tradition,* Vol. XX, No. 2 (Summer 1995). Lyrics from "Garden Party" by Rick Nelson copyright © 1972 Matragun Music. Lyrics from "Dracula Moon" by Joan Osborne, Eric Bazilian, Rob Hyman & Rick Chertoff © 1995 Human Boy Music (ASCAP), Dub Notes (ASCAP), & Monkey in the Middle Music (ASCAP). All Rights o/b/o Human Boy Music and Dub Notes administered by WB Music Corp. All Rights Reserved. Used by Permission. "Dracula Moon" also copyrighted © 1995 Songs of PolyGram International, Inc., Womanly Hips Music, and Monkey In The Middle Music (and as designated by co-publishers). Used by Permission. All Rights Reserved.

ISBN 0-553-57576-7

Published simultaneously in the United States and Canada

Bantam Books are published by Bantam Books, a division of Bantam Doubleday Dell Publishing Group, Inc. Its trademark, consisting of the words "Bantam Books" and the portrayal of a rooster, is Registered in U.S. Patent and Trademark Office and in other countries. Marca Registrada. Bantam Books, 1540 Broadway, New York, New York 10036.

PRINTED IN THE UNITED STATES OF AMERICA

OPM 10 9 8 7 6 5 4 3 2 1

To my parents, who were amazing: This is ten years too late but better than never.

The word stranger *denotes a living embodiment of that which is strange—from the Old French,* estranger, *extraordinary. Thus, the stranger functions as an unexpected messenger who can embody or mirror what is extraordinary within us, what is possible but yet unlived.*

—From "The Bridge of Well-Being" by Mark Nepo

PROLOGUE

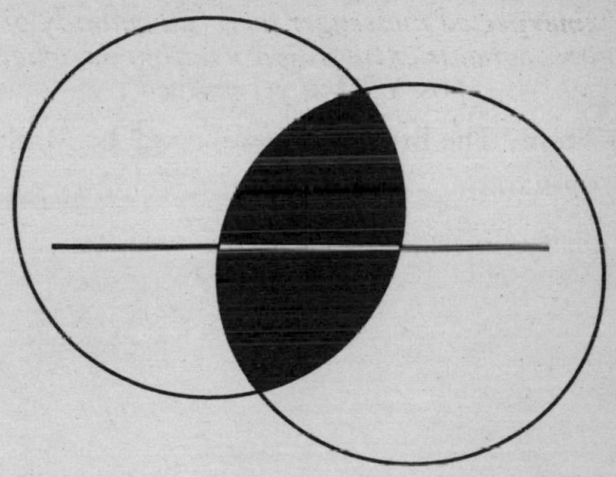

The signature reality of growing older: either be haunted by something or surrender your heart to the darkness of not giving a damn.

—Unknown Twen-Cen Philosopher

I dream of old people gambling, playing baccarat while they die, the perfect glitter of the casino in stark neon contrast to the corruption of their flesh. There is sweet irony in defying the certainty of death with games of chance, as if the money matters, as if winning were possible in the face of odds stacked like chips in favor of the house. Before death and resurrection there is chance, there is luck. There is the possibility of God, however frightening a divine wisdom who created such as this, this grand glittering pasture of lights and naked showgirls, this illusion of beauty and wealth where old people go to becomes its victims . . .

There is purity; then there is me, twisting on satin

sheets under the cool hiss of climate-controlled air dreaming of mortal things, of money that matters. Of God.

There is an odd juxtaposition here, a telepath dreaming of thoughts she can normally hear but doesn't want to. I dream because I wonder: Have I defied God by my talents, my abilities, my bolstered immune system? Have I become more *of* him because of the luck of the draw—there but for the grace goes I? *Old. Gambling. Dying.*

Pray for resurrection from the roll of the dice. I am a powerful telepath, capable of lifting residual thoughts from dead flesh, made wealthy because I solved a crime, solved a criminal and ripped off a fortune. Sweet irony that this criminal was killing to provide me with the key to life. He died providing me with a bolstered immune system and the money to enjoy longevity. I'd spent years looking into the heads of corpses trying to coax some clue as to their killers, to assess the role of chance in their murders. It was rarely chance, rare that victim and killer weren't involved in some deadly dance of flaws and maneuvers.

Now that I am wealthy I dream, and the horror of murder postmortem pales in comparison to what happens when I dream of old people gambling, the role of the dice. The bitter chance of agony. My devil and my god inside me, rolled into one in my head, impaling me on the amplitude spikes of his brain waves. His evil the chance that God takes for creating the world, his evil a dark stain, washing over me, staining the sheets with my sweat, here he comes, *here he comes . . .*

He pursues her through the crowd, a throng, actually, the bodies packed tightly together in a place with warm sunshine and not so bad smog. He is grinning, pushing people aside and getting looks of fear in return. He doesn't want them, however. He wants her, glimpsed thirty feet in front of him, shapely legs and sandaled feet, short hair, shorts, moving politely through the crowd with no knowledge of the danger thrashing through the men, women, and children to overtake her.

He closes the gap, heart rate increasing, an errant thought—<I can't take her here>—*and a hard-core response to what "taking her" means.*

—a hand on her arm, and the perspective shifts, she is now turning toward the pressure of his grip—

—his hand clamped over her mouth in the middle of hundreds of people, a finger to his lips to silence her—

—fear, hers, wide-eyed vision of her would-be attacker, a wiry man with muscles and a sick grin, her strength no match for his, for his . . .

—desire. Enhanced by the public though silent struggle, the crowd not noticing the action because they are invisible to them on a rare warm sunny day. The other hand—

—roughly pawing her breasts, obscenely tweaking her nipple so that it hurts, the minor pain manipulated by terror, her voice silenced by his other hand, mirrored sunglasses, tattoo on his arm—

And it stops there, but the residuals from his thoughts leave no doubt as to what's coming. The man with the sunglasses is always the same, the same churning in his mind so accessible to me.

The victims are always different, always attractive and alone, their reactions heartbreakingly similar, also accessible through me.

* * *

I do not know their names, this stranger and his victims.

I have no sense of where they are, but they are way beyond the normal range of a capable's thought reception. The tableaus block out all of the background babble, and this stranger acts his impulses frequently. I am powerless to stop him, powerless to defend myself against his thoughts. It's as if I share each assault from both sides, as if I am both rapist and victim in the same shallow breath.

And I know that he has some other purpose, some deeper resonance to his impulses than the power of defilement . . .

. . . when I wake up with sore and aching thighs, I know this stranger has replayed the parts that he doesn't let me see real time, replayed them to my subconscious while I sleep, so that I may more fully play along as the victim, so that this stranger can fuck me, too. Again, and again, and again.

Ironic that I'm not that experienced in carnal matters. Since I discovered my telepathic talents the discordant thoughts of normals sicken me; I am intimate with the world within a thirty-foot radius whether I like it or not. Achieving greater intimacy is like trying to find the deepest part of the sewer. And as the stranger shows, the deepest part of the sewer usually finds me. So he takes me when I am asleep, when I dream . . .

I am not Jenny anymore. A part of me has died under his assault. Instead I am vigilant, waiting, watching for the wiry man with mirrored sunglasses and the serpent's tattoo on his arm. I know that my stranger is waiting, too, waiting to unleash all of his hatred upon me at the moment of confrontation, hatred expressed through the numbing fear of his brutal conquests. I fear he will break me before I can get to him, before I can tear his fucking heart from his chest and wipe the blood and gristle on his face.

A young woman in the wrong place at the wrong time, people around but no one watching, no one but me, no one but me. The chips swept away and the woman crumbles into nothing, nothing, and no one notices, the rapist drags her into the woods, tears clothing, no one notices, bad *luck?* Bad luck to be in harm's way, to be young and twisted into a man's plaything, cruel chance, cruel sweat on the sheets, surrounded by money that doesn't matter, all the money in the world, all the winning bets a sham. Guilt, who can feel guilty in the face of this defilement? I feel victim's guilt, codependence, the secret thrill of illicit sex, of shame mixed with excitement mixed with fear, a meltdown in this sudden loss of identity, this catastrophic loss of self, this sense of being *taken.*

This is my nightmare nested in a telepathic vision, terror I understand all too well, repetition I cannot stop. He's not looking for me, he doesn't want me, he just wants me to know, just wants me to play along, play along and know him, know what he does. He's not a telepath, this stranger, he's just dialed into me somehow, maybe just a latent broadcaster, maybe no connection between the two of us at all. So I am trapped. A fucked-up thrill like bondage (who's piggybacking now?), more guilty because I'm not the victim of this man's theater, more guilty because other people's pain provides me with this . . . *entertainment.* Here he comes, here he comes, while I sleep, *here he comes . . .*

To free myself, I must kill the stranger. I must kill that part of myself that lives in fear.

BOOK ONE

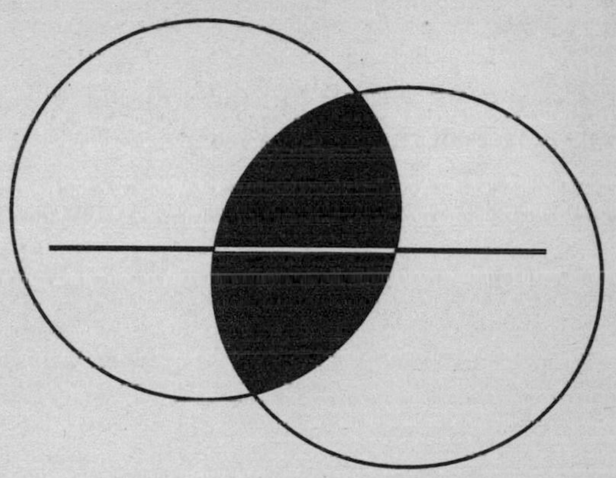

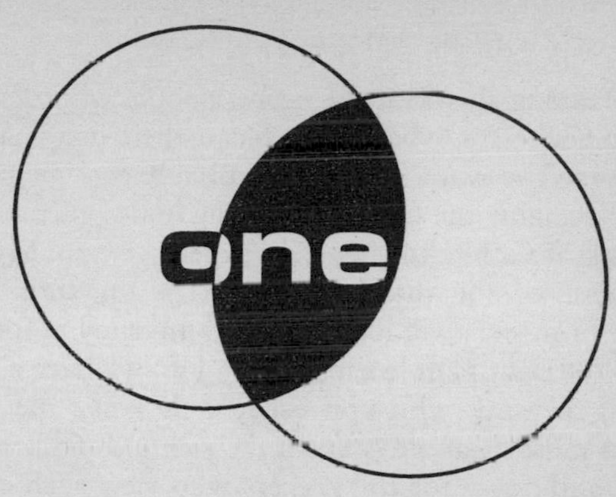

Los Angeles, California—December 24, 2052

My home sits in the Hollywood Hills, custom-designed and built in the two years since I inherited money, lots of money, lots of land. The driveway is two lanes of blacktop that stretches from my gate on county property for half a mile before the main villa. The guards are heavily armed with assault choppers for backup should the rabble get curious; a small army ensures that I never rub shoulders with anyone I don't want to. It seems paranoid, you say, but this is Los Angeles for the wealthy living in a remote part of town, the essence of nouveau riche is to talk about contingency plans for hostage taking and terrorist situations.

Tonight is a party. My turn on the social calendar amid the matrons and the captains of industry who are my newfound friends, and my spread has to be more elaborate than the most stunning soiree they could imagine. There are people who make seven figures a year planning this kind of event, people who demand carte blanche for whatever tableau their imaginations configure. The waterfall effect probably cost me plenty just in changing the facade of the big house, plenty for a gimmick. It's a bitch being rich; expensive, too. My bud Betty assured me that it wouldn't be my turn for a decade or more, a gig like this guarantees my in for that long if the right people show up and if they have a good time, if they ask who you used, if they like the food. Success must mean envy from the rich old biddies who attend and pussy for the geezers who view such events as a break from having to pay for it.

The opening gambit for this madness is the waterfall. Not just water but special catalysts whose formula has been given to the dressmakers and tailors for the rich and famous so that they may fashion something appropriate for their clients who will be attending. My planner has a whole staff hacking into those people's databases, tracking who commissioned evening wear for my party, who has picked up, and who has paid. The numbers are good. The demographics of the "A" list who have confirmed pickups and payments is very good. People are coming to my party. Important, rich people. I have arrived.

I stand in front of the fifteen-foot-high ice fountain sculpted in my image sipping some of the champagne that spouts from between my icy legs. A private joke, all things considered, as the staff swings into action. I can only watch and wait at this point, the plans and the reputations are all on the line, watch and wait as the first guest steps from a mag-lev limo in front and walks toward the waterfall. Toward me.

Carol Madigan, supermodel. A holographic image of her stepping out of her limousine in a long slinky dress is projected on my side of the waterfall. She mugs for the pickup, models slyly. Steps into the waterfall.

Appears on the other side in a thong bikini. The catalysts in the water break down the polymers in her evening dress, shearing it away to reveal what's underneath. Well the gimmick works. And she's a slut, invited for that very purpose.

"Jen!" she greets me too brightly. Someone hands her a towel for her auburn hair. (At five feet nine inches, blond, green eyes, great body, I'm pretty attractive. But next to six feet one inch of Carol Madigan with her violet eyes and high cheekbones and body so sculpted a bite of graham cracker would double her bra size, I look like a fucking boy. On the really dark days I could give her the "sledgehammer cure.") I hand her a champagne glass that she eagerly accepts, then sputters laughing as she sees the ice sculpture and the flow from between its legs. I just shove my glass under the stream for a refill.

"That time of the month," I say coyly, my lines rehearsed with speech writers who could just as easily get me elected madam president of our great nation. Each guest will get a different repartee from the stored data implanted in my head.

The next guest passes through the waterfall, winding up in his birthday suit, a wrinkled old codger too rich to give a damn. Entrance slots have also been more closely scripted than landings at Los Angeles International and published to the guests. He clearly has designs on Madigan, and she clearly would screw a banister in his house just to get close. A perfect pair.

They go off together, and the evening begins as it is supposed to.

* * *

The guests come in. Somewhere in the basement the support staff have the processors running on overtime and the holographic before waterfall images of the guests are computer-animated with lifelike movement and actually join the party. More guests, more holographic images, more animation, more traffic problems to keep the guests and the imagery from running into each other and spoiling the illusion. Hell, I'm having a problem keeping to my own script with the guests, and I have this Forbidden Planet image of Krell machinery keening away in the basement, dials alight as more and more processing power comes on-line.

Someone whispers into the processor at the base of my skull, *<one more body and the sims will fucking **crash**>* and I want to hold my breath. The great court of my house is full of people and their doppelgängers. The more vain are conversing with themselves. The more stupid are hitting on a "warm body" that is nothing more than unusually coherent laser light. And then the lights dim.

The last limo in the holding pattern has long since been cleared to land. All the guests are here. The holograms are retreating to the waterfall, slipping away, disengaging from the crowds. Finally, when they are all lined up, a single pure white light finds me in the crowd.

I clear my throat, making sure the parabolic mike is centered. The sound pipes in over the loudspeaker system, the background talk begins fading.

"Ladies and gentlemen," I begin, not surprised by the sound of my voice coming from the speakers, "I want to welcome you to my house, and the world's first virtual party."

The holographic images begin clapping, the sound seems real, the images processed to perfection. Phosphorescence dumped into the waterfall begins glowing, backlighting the digital images of everyone at the party. An impressed murmur moves through the guests. The holograms seemingly join hands and begin to bow—

<who the fuck is he?> comes the sudden cry over the network humming in my head, drowning out my next lines. One, no, two people are emerging through the waterfall. The external pickups are forming a new holographic image of them both—

<oh, shit! we just kicked it right over the edge!> followed by an artificially constructed voice:

<FATAL SYSTEM ERROR>

as the last image flickers to life, a familiar hunch to its shoulders. Too much, the Krell machinery goes off-line in the basement, the magnificent holographic sims of the legitimate guests flicker and wink out of existence.

LAPD Detective Derrick Trent stands there in a soaking wet tuxedo staring at a half-formed image of himself.

His girlfriend's black roots are showing in her wet, slick bleached blond hair.

"Nice of you to crash my party, Derrick. Literally."

"The waterfall gag's a nice touch, Jenny. But a 'hi, how'ya doin' ' would have been sufficient."

Derrick Trent, LAPD: We go back twelve years, back to when I was a piggybacker, back to when I was running around using telepathy to help him nail perps. He rescued me from piggybacking, a form of mind rental that allows your client to do kinky things with your body.

"Hmm. What, exactly, brings you here?"

"It's been six months since I talked to you. Almost two years since the Waters case. Thought tonight might be the perfect opportunity to get reacquainted."

"These things take weeks of planning. It's like a military maneuver, chum. You walked in on the critical part of the formation and fucked it up."

He just looks at me. "You sleeping okay, Jen?"

Shit . . . I don't meet his eyes. "Yeah, sure. Fine."

He looks into my eyes anyway. "You don't look it. Morph makeup hides a lot. But not everything. Not to me."

"Drop it, Trent." Morph makeup is the latest from the money-crazed cosmetics industry. Nanotech in a jar, expensive as hell. Burn victims swear by it. The subcutaneous variety is even programmable.

Derrick starts to say something smart, then backs off. "Yeah, sure. You still using Sytogene?"

Sytogene is a drug that turns my telepathy off. For capables, it's the analogue of Masque that inhibits thought projection by normals.

"In a crowd like this, what do you think?"

"To your eyeballs, I'd say."

"I'll drink to that." I push my glass under the champagne piss coming through my ice-sculptured legs.

Derrick just looks at the ice statue and shakes his head. His girlfriend—Maida?—is off talking to some playboy type.

"Who's tonight's cheap thrill?" I ask, inclining my head toward his date.

"Been seeing her for about six weeks."

"True love, eh?"

"Nope. A substitute for the real thing."

"She needs a better hairdresser."

"She likes that look. Retro and all. Does it herself."

Ugh, chemicals. "And you like the look, too?"

He shrugs. Derrick is tentative, uncertain of himself. Since I'm nuked I can't pick up what he's thinking, but things haven't been the same since our last case together. I miss it, in a way.

"Anything interesting crossing the wire?"

"What? Oh, sure. Lots of good stuff. Between the zone and the Stim fiends, the body count has become a problem."

Ah, homicide. But curiosity gets the better of me. I ask it as casually as I can. "Anything concerning a series of rapes?"

"Not that I know of. But I'm homicide. I wouldn't get involved anyway."

"Right." But his cop's antennae are up and waving in the air, sniffing.

"Something you want me to check out?"

I'd prefer it if my nightmares weren't real. "No. Nothing."

He looks at me with that old Derrick look. But says nothing.

Among the guests is a man who looks familiar. Very familiar. He is medium build, thin, six feet two inches tall, dark hair with a bit of gray, stylish, really. He is in animated conversation with a merely wealthy plastic surgeon, a Beverly Hills staple. I swirl around their discussion, eavesdropping.

". . . but the fundamentalists with this back to the strict interpretations of the Bible and the Constitution would simply make things worse."

The doctor, his back to me: "I don't see how things could get much worse. No one's safe. They can't keep everything bottled up in the zone forever. Hell, liberals and their interpretations of the Constitution created the problems. I say if it isn't there, it shouldn't be interpreted to be there. The fundamentalists just want to get back to what's real."

"The South Central Zone is not something ordained by the Bible or the Constitution. Not in any sense of either document."

"What about the death penalty?"

"Which one? The state-sanctioned execution or the near certainty of catching a fatal communicable disease in prison?"

"I mean an eye for an eye." The doctor swigs champagne. His companion isn't drinking, I notice.

"You forget 'vengence is mine, sayeth the lord.' "

"And you forget the reasons why the zone was erected in the first place."

The stranger smiles. "Didn't you agree to the concept of the South Central Zone when it was created?"

"Sure. Most people did."

"What about the people living in South Central? Think they agreed?"

"*They* are the problem. Who cares what they think?"

"You can't have it both ways. Nothing in the Constitution suggests that incarcerating whole segments of the population is legal. You want fundamentalism? Or do you want to ignore all the parts of the Bill of Rights that are troublesome? When did we make the leap of faith from 'law and order' to police state? What has it gotten us?"

"I shudder to think what things would be like without the zone. Those people . . . free to wander the streets . . . no telling what horrors they'd perpetrate."

"Assuming they still had their constitutional rights, correct, Doctor?"

"Freedom isn't free. There's a price to it. In South Central, the price is a loss of democratic institutions."

I sense my chance to break in. "And what price are we paying, Doctor?"

"Jenny, hi. You tell me." The good doctor waves his glass in the air to emphasize his point. "You probably keep a small army of security forces—it probably costs you a small fortune."

"Despite the fact that most of the blacks are bottled up in South Central."

"If they weren't, no amount of money would make you feel safe."

No amount of money makes me feel safe, anyway. I turn to the familiar stranger. I like the twinkle in his eyes.

"And what do you think?" I ask. Trying desperately to place the face without calling up a recognition program from the microprocessor buried at the base of my neck.

"I think God would find our society wanting." He smiles. He knows who I am. Why can't I place him?

I tilt my head quizzically. "I know you, don't I?"

"I'd say so, Jenny. Mitch. Mitch Belford. From about one hundred years ago."

Mitch. Met him just after high school. He's changed, as if only the shell of his present self was around when I met him.

From when I slept with him. One time. My first consensual sex. My last.

"You're right. It's been a century." *Holy shit,* and the earth moves beneath me. Not because of that, silly. I met Mitch when I was young, confused, and had repressed a lot of things that I wouldn't recover until years later.

He nods. "I see you've done well."

"And what about you?" And how did you get invited to my exclusive party if you aren't a mover and shaker?"

"I've been around."

"Meaning?"

"Meaning I'd like to talk about old times, Jenny. Plenty of time to catch up to the present, at least I hope so."

"Old times." I can sense his appraising look, the kind I routinely get from men. I don't mind it from him, but I can't make myself give him the once-over. Not even for old times.

"I always knew you were special. I also knew that you and I would never last."

"At least you were right about the second part." *He was the only guy I ever trusted enough to let touch me. But even then . . .*

"Ships in the night."

"Yeah. Ships in the night." We "hove to" just long enough to fuck. Like the sex could fill in the void in who I was, but it couldn't, it never could. And I remembered other things that weren't so pleasant, maybe a glimmer here or there, like an image you keep seeing but is never there when you turn toward it. *Like a beach. And a boy.*

"Do you see anyone from the old days?"

Oh, Mitch. So much has happened, none of it simple to explain. "No. No one." *And a power . . .*

"Neither do I."

"Then how did you get an invitation to my exclusive party?"

He smiles.

"I'm a priest."

I take an involuntary step back and remember his coolly sexual appraisal. "A priest."

"Recently left the priesthood. Very recently."

"But why come to my party?"

"You invited me because of my former position. I was chief prefect of the Church of the Resurrection here on the West Coast."

The Church of the Resurrection. Wealthier than the Catholic Church in these parts even with a much smaller following.

"Yet you left the church?"

"My choice was not rash, nor was it without pain."

There is an easily ascertainable depth to his words, nothing as simple as pain or remorse, but deeper, a crisis of identity reaching to his very core. I decide to leave that to a time when I wasn't tranked and could listen to him on all levels.

We resolve to keep in touch, to have lunch. Our hands brush and I am struck that his flesh against mine doesn't dredge up memories of our former intimacy.

The party winds down and the destruction is impressively consistent with people having a good time. The small army of staffers working the party are replaced by a relief force that will clean all this shit up. At dawn the last guest has been breakfasted and ushered out; the last bedroom has been emptied and the sheets changed, the sanitized ones marked off with yellow police tape to keep the horny fuckers out. The last mag-lev limo is trailing clean nonpolluting exhaust into the California sunshine.

Elmo, my party planner, is going through the postmortem, chiding me about Derrick Trent ruining the virtual party effect, as if I should somehow control the riffraff in my past if I'm to work with him again. After all, the system folding up is more a reflection upon his reputation than mine; it's funny the way half the room simply vaporized the minute Derrick swam through the falls with noncomforming threads, his expression more big dumb "Huh?" than he should be given credit for.

At this point I should sleep, but I don't want to dream of old people, nor do I want to fall prey to the mysterious stranger who haunts my rest. Wish that I could walk through a waterfall and experience rebirth as something or someone different, morphed into someone with a more pleasing or confident background and more than enough social graces to go with scads of money. Wish that a waterfall could cleanse my sins or at least prepare me for new ones, wish that I could wash away my coming addiction to telepathy deadening drugs. I can't stand to be around my "friends" and hear their inner voices anymore. Too banal, too envious, too petty, as if I were dulling the blades of my talent by banging it against a dull rock. I look out into the sunshine filling my bedroom, at a dawn sweeter for me because I have all of *this* and will continue to have it for the rest of my very long life. The last thing I think as I finally drift off is a curse—

<lucky me> because I have it all, and you damn sure don't.

And I know that nature abhors inequity as much as it abhors a vacuum.

* * *

Derrick Trent calls me sometime during the feverish day after the party. The fact that it happens to be Christmas is irrelevant—Christmas happens every day when you are rich and alone. It takes him fifteen minutes to convince my house operator that he's not some hack soliciting tix for the policemen's ball. Or so he says. Actually, fifteen would indicate that he's an incredibly skilled hostage negotiator, given what I tell the help about unwanted disturbances.

"Jen, it's about time. Look, I know you're out of commission, but I really need to get you involved in something."

"How much?"

He laughs. "It's not about money, Jen. It's a mystery. This one will go away if I can't get some private help. No constituency to help foot the bill."

"A mystery." The notion takes a while to filter through my synapses.

"A body. On ice. Waiting for that Jenny Sixa touch. We need some answers on this one, Jenny. Need 'em bad."

"Who? Where?"

"I can have a bird over your head in ten. You do have a helipad somewhere on that spread, don't you?"

"Yup. Sure. Answer my questions."

"It's a kid. Found in the subway at Hollywood Boulevard. Dead. And this isn't the first time that something like this has happened."

A child. "Who is it?"

"White male, age about fifteen. ID is gonna be a problem. C'mon, Jenny."

Derrick's voice is low, urgent. *ID is gonna be a problem. Shit. Merry Christmas, kid.*

My resistance to getting involved in a case is low

right now. I don't know why. I just had the party to end all parties. I belong. It's been two years since I strapped on a homicide investigation.

But a fifteen-year-old is a homicide victim somewhere in Los Angeles. Happens all the time, I'd wager. Why me? Why now?

"Jen?"

"Why me, Derrick? Is this why you crashed my party?"

"Jen, we have the body packed in ice waiting for you. Do you understand? Department doesn't even sanction telepaths on this kind of case. I'm hanging out here exposed."

"Why me, dammit?"

"Trust me. You'll see. Trust me."

He needs me to get in there, take a look, and get out. This is the twenty-first century where justice has to be purchased by people with big enough checkbooks. Ordinary people are encouraged to die unobtrusively, thank you very much. If you be poor, maybe you get a beat cop saying "that's a damn shame, ma'am," when one of the chilluns kicks. Try choking that down with your morning coffee, sweets.

Fifteen years old.

Dead.

A mystery. Not the first time.

"I'll meet the chopper on my pad. Just have him make it quick, 'kay?"

"Sure, Jen, sure. Thanks."

Yeah, sure, you fuck. Thank *you*.

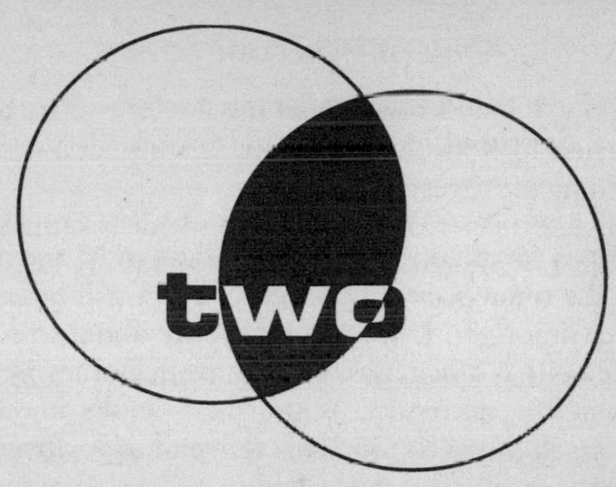

I find that my trips to hell are too quick and too frequent. I'm picked up and deposited near the crime scene in minutes. My system is clear of Sytogene, and the pilot's thoughts come through clear as a bell. Christ, I hate this.

My eyes are frosty with not-ready-to-fall tears, walking difficult under the weight of fatigue. Derrick Trent leads me into the city subway past an old black man singing and playing guitar on the outskirts of the yellow police "crime scene" tape. They've packed the body in ice to try to preserve the brain chemistry, so that I can try to connect with the victim's last thoughts. This bizarre talent is the reason why I made tons o' cash, and the reason I ran away from it once my future was financially secure.

The subway platform is dank and humid with rat-scurrying smells and sounds, and the old black man sings:

"I went to a garden party
To reminisce with my old friends . . ."

before I lose the rest of the lyrics in his West Indian accent. He is too funky and too harmless to be moved to secure the crime scene. The fact that he's still here singing is testimony to LAPD's indifference about this case.

The body is a teenager, head shaven, clothes plain to the point of anonymity. White male, looks about fifteen. I reach down to touch his shaven head, closing my eyes to the smells and the humidity and my own trauma from the night before, squeeze my eyes so tightly shut that a few hot tears compress through my lashes and run down my cheeks. The boy's thoughts are blank, not empty but blank, a sheer wall of smooth stone, undimpled by any feature, uneroded by any emotional weather. At first I'm not convinced that there is anything left for me to experience until the cracks appear and the vision of his thoughts begins to corrupt and break down. Even in decay there is nothing there, nothing, his mind as smooth as a newborn's.

As I resurface I hear the old man strumming the same two cords, singing faster:

"A chance to share old memories
and play our songs again . . ."

and Derrick looks at me as I shake my head, nothing. Not a clue.

"When I got to the garden party
they all knew my name
But no one recognized me
I didn't look the same . . ."

"We called you because his prints and retinals aren't on file."

"What?" Impossible, of course, because everyone is bagged and tagged at birth. You can't not be in the system. You can't be a stranger to the net.

"You heard me. No records. Nothing that suggests who John Doe here is. That plus his age makes it a problem."

"Sure." Babies showing up dead in the subway with no one to claim them was a problem. Babies, civilians, noncoms with no identity in the battlefield was somehow frightening to officialdom, to the notions of control and would never, ever, do.

"So you saw nothing?"

"No . . . How was he killed?"

"Injection, looks like, if it's consistent with the first body. We never tried to ascertain cause of death for the first one, but I will use my juice to get the coroner to give us a full report on both corpses. We're also gonna take tissue samples and see if we can somehow match him to a DNA database, but that's a long shot." DNA is a long shot. Nobody's giving up free samples of genetic material these days. Too easy for it to show up in unusual and embarrassing places.

"What about his hand?" He has a mark on his right palm, a wound of some sort.

"I'll get the coroner to take a look. Probably not the cause of death, though. Possibly not even related to the cause of death because there's no evidence of bleeding or anything. Just a flesh wound."

Trent stops me as we break into sunlight aboveground. Behind me I can hear the old man strumming and singing off-key:

"But it's all right now,
I learned my lesson well,
You see you can't please everyone
so you got to please yourself."

"What's with you?" He moves to smudge the tracks of my tears.

"Partying too much, I guess."

"Sleep at all last night?" Derrick pops a stick of gum in his mouth as I light a cigarette. Bastard Trent quit six months ago and shows every sign of making it.

"A little," I say and turn toward the too bright sunshine. Derrick sighs behind me, and I hear his mind, *<christ, Jenny>* as he allows himself to care one last time.

"Nice party," he says conversationally. His thoughts rearrange themselves around his new, antismoking health-nut girlfriend with black roots to make room for me.

"Hit the jackpot, y'know. Busy spending money."

"So I've heard." Wild parties in the Hollywood Hills are indeed my new forte. Too much money from the last case, too many problems unleashed from the lack of a credit deficit that used to be problem numero uno. No problem to do a little pro bono for Detective Trent and the LAPD, no problem at all. Maybe desperate to escape my gilded cage, in fact, and the stranger that invades my thoughts when I'm not looking.

"Sorry I couldn't be any help here."

"Oh, right. Second one of these kinds of corpses that've turned up in the last month. Strangers. Nothing in the computers. No identities. Young kids, too, they look about fifteen. Weird."

"Anybody got much interest in solving these?"

"In the department? Nah. Nothing to justify the overhead of looking. All we do is put out enough PR to keep the locals from getting nervous." He takes my arm. "I was hoping you'd be interested in picking up some of the slack."

He looks at me from the corner of his eye, and I can hear his thoughts, *<you need a distraction, Jen>*

And for once, the lunkhead just might be right.

I haven't been to my office in months. It seems odd walking into the lobby at such an unusual hour, it's about 10:45 in the morning. I take the elevator up to the appropriate floor, gaze for a moment at the lettering on the door:

Jenny Sixa
Capable
Private Investigations

and push on through.

"Boss!" Didi, my automaton secretary/girl Friday/assistant leaps from her keyboard and hugs me. I haven't seen her in months, either, although I know she's been attending to business and keeping things shipshape because that's what my Deeds would do.

"Hey, Deeds," I say sheepishly as I lay my tote on the guest chair in the empty foyer of my office. Didi gives me the once-over.

Shakes her head. "Boss, you look like shit. Coffee?" This last she asks brightly as if she violated some mechanical protocol in callin' 'em like she sees 'em.

I slump wearily into a chair. "I feel like shit, Deeds."

She hands me a cup of insta brew that is just as awful as I remember. "Ugh, at least score some cappuccino from the machine in the hall, Deeds."

"Right, boss."

As she leaves I look at the office, taking time to peek into my inner sanctum. The place is clean, well kept, even though there can't have been much going on in my extended absence. Although I find it odd that there are files on my desk. Fresh files.

Didi returns and hands me a cup of cappuccino. "How's business?" I ask her, my eyebrow raised quizzically.

"Um, good! I mean, really slow. Nobody calls anymore, since you haven't been . . ."

The phone chimes, then the second line chimes as well.

". . . in." Then she leaps to the phones. And I can just imagine what manner of hustle this is. As it turns out, the place has been humming without me.

"Gee, boss, it seemed stupid to sit here and answer the phone and tell people you were rich and didn't know if you were coming back to work because you didn't need money anymore."

"So you did the next best thing."

"Right. I started taking simple cases that didn't need you. Computer stuff. Skip traces. Anything that didn't require too much personal interaction with the clients."

"Who'd you get to play me? When you had to, I mean."

"Oh, I did. I kept the meetings with people short and made sure that I was dressed like a human. And I learned to act gruff and grumpy."

"Like humans."

"Uh-huh."

"Make any money?"

Didi looks at the floor and doesn't respond immediately.

"Okay, did you lose a lot of money?"

"No. Made money. Lots, actually."

"Really." Now this is amusing. I specialized in high-profile, difficult-to-solve cases where there was a payoff for working with the LAPD. When you solved one you were golden, but the down times used to be really bad. Used to be.

"Yeah. It's all in the bank, 'cept for the bills I paid."

"The rent, your salary, things like that."

"Yup. Let me show you the figures."

And she shows me. Poor girl hasn't taken anything for herself I see, and the bank balance is, wow, actually impressive.

That's a lot of skip traces and computer noodling.

"Boss?"

"Yes, Deeds?"

"Are you back?"

"I'm not sure. Maybe for a while. Why?"

"Can I keep my cases?"

Looking at her, listening to the phone ringing off the hook, I am struck by how much the enterprise is more hers than mine. There is a distinct sense of loss there, somewhere.

Oh, well.

"What do you think?" We are admiring the handiwork on the door. It says:

Didi Myers & Jenny Sixa
Artificial Capable

Private Investigations

"Looks good to me. You sure you don't want top billing, boss?"

"Nope. Just want a place to hang my hat when I want to get back into the swing of things."

"I like it."

"It's really your business now, Deeds. And I guess you'll have to stop calling me boss."

"Hmm. Okay. But what do I call you?"

"How about Jenny?"

She giggles at the thought, but we shake on it right there.

After she quiets she asks me: "So what are we working on?"

"Derrick called me on this one. Two cases of young men, no more than fifteen, found dead without any evidence that they exist. No identifiers in the net, retinals, fingerprints, nothing."

"Any possibility that they'd been surgically altered?"

"Anything's possible. But not likely. And who would go through the trouble just to kill the product?"

"Someone who thought they weren't needed anymore."

"Yes, but why?"

"Wait a sec, boss. Both decedents were around the same age?"

"That's what Derrick said. He should be squirting a datafile shortly."

"What if they got too old to be useful?"

"Useful for what?"

"That's what we have to find out."

"Hmm. Maybe. That would imply that someone is creating kids and keeping them off the net from birth."

"In vitro fertilization."

"What?"

"Artificial fertilization of a female ovum outside of the womb. It's a popular fertility technique."

"It's also monstrous, if you think about it. Who would create kids? And what would these people do with them?"

"Kill them if they didn't work out, maybe?"

"Whew, gives me the shivers. Let's go inside, partner."

"Sureboss."

Derrick's datafile arrives and I am staring at the haunting face of the first fifteen-year-old white male, also, according to Derrick, deceased via lethal injection. His head is shaved, his eyelids slightly open, like a dull-witted boy half-asleep for the camera. His face is utterly devoid of expression, not even peaceful, but empty, as empty as John Doe 2's mind had been earlier that day. This one has no records, no priors. A tiny pinprick killed him, and unlike John Doe 2 he has a puncture wound on his left foot.

Derrick and LAPD have to come up with something to get us started. Even if the case isn't supported by some big shot paying for their computer time, they need to give me something.

Anything.

Derrick calls me late, surprised to find me in the office.

"What's Myers and Sixa?"

"The new reality, Derrick. Didi has been running things in my absence and she's got a good little business going. Didi Myers, that is."

"Oh, so that's her last name. I never knew."

Neither did I.

"Anyway, Jen, seems we got real lucky."

"You have the perp. Case closed. The world is safe for democracy again."

"No. We got an extremely lucky match on the DNA side."

"How so?"

"The people involved are Feds. Federal Bureau of Investigation. Their genetic markers are required to be on file for identification in case one of 'em gets blown up or something."

"There's more than one involved?"

"No. He is one Robert Conyers, Special Agent in Charge, Los Angeles County Anti-Terrorist Office. The 'they' is his wife, uh, Susan. She has old oil money."

"So what's the connection between John Doe 2 and these people?"

"Ah, this is the good part. John Doe 2 appears to have been her son."

"Hers? But not his?"

"You win the lotto, missy. Lucky we fucked up on programming the search, otherwise we'd have never found them."

"What's your next step?"

Derrick chuckles. "Hey, if the Fibbies want to have illegitimate kids that's their business, Jen."

"Not even a phone call to suggest that they not litter the landscape with their unwanted progeny, Derrick?"

"Give me a break, Jen. You know the Fibbies. Those

fucking people are ball busters! Particularly the women. Piss one of them off and you're knee deep in some counterterrorist conspiracy investigation on departmental graft or something. Sorry, I don't need the hassle."

"Or the paperwork."

"Yeah, uh-huh. Look, Jen, somebody's gonna start waving the bill for the computer time in my face, so let's just say that I'm turning this one over to you. Call me if you need anything, but none of this came from me, okay?"

"Fine. How's the new girlfriend? Get her to a decent hairdresser yet?"

Derrick tilts his head. "Nice of you to ask," he says, and cuts the circuit without answering the question.

Now if I could just figure out why I keep asking him about her . . .

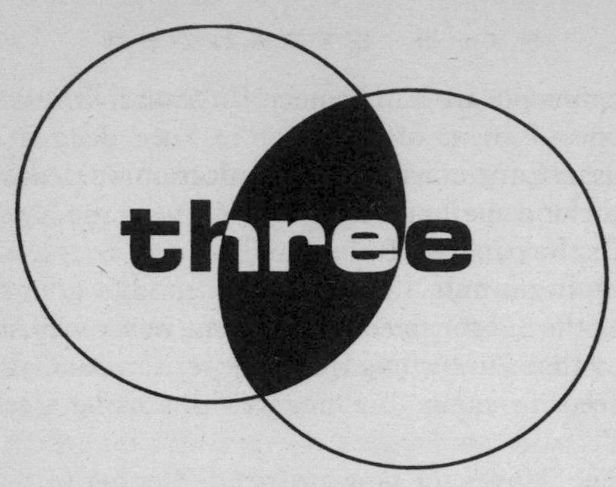

three

So I had a name. With a name came an address. I could stay home the day after Christmas, or I could go sleuthing. Hire a car to get me to their address. They lived in Santa Barbara, admittedly a bit more than "drop in" distance from LA, but what the hey.

The house, the community, had the kind of uptight neatness that is more like compulsion than good grooming. Madness lived behind these picket fences and ran free on those expansive lawns, wives with nothing to do except go quietly insane as busy important husbands called them ungrateful for fucking up the lives only good men could provide them.

The Conyerses had a nice little bungalow, a nice little life with good neighbors still untouched by anything but the juvenile crimes of passionate youth. I had this image of the two of them, clean-cut and square, sipping martinis over the back fence of the 'hood, talking with the neighbors about the cost of college or sports or the local PTA. I admit this image was way into the resentful scales, but I'm rich, remember? At least it wasn't about money.

Susan Conyers answered the door. "Yes?" she asked from behind the screen.

"I'm looking for Robert and Mrs. Conyers?" I said, smiling sweetly.

"I'm Susan Conyers. Robert is away on business." Her hands never approached the screen door. She was shortish, five feet five inches, going dumpy slowly.

"I'd very much like to talk to you, then, Mrs. Conyers."

She sighed, looking at me closely through the mesh. "Look, if you've come with some tearful confession about sleeping with my husband during some messed-up stakeout in East LA, forget about it. That's a trip I've already taken too many times with women who looked just as good and were even younger. Okay? Have we satisfied Your Courage in Coming to Confess?"

"Sorry, I've never met your husband. I wish it were about someone *he's* schtupping."

<she looks harmless enough> she thinks, and I relax. Getting in isn't going to be difficult.

Susan Conyers opened the screen door. I stop short at the snub black needle gun she holds in her hands because it's pointed right at my stomach.

She looked down at the gun in her hands. "Ooops! Sorry. Sometimes the strumpets get a little huffy." She casually places the gun on the kitchen counter and lets me in.

"I hope I didn't scare you," she said, even though she kinda frightened the piss out of me.

False bravado one-oh-one: "Nope. My gun is bigger. See?" I'd had my hand on my pistol the whole time. Instincts die hard, you understand.

Susan Conyers threw back her head and laughed. "Just think, honey, we could've been blazing away over an Avon lady visit or something. No, I don't have your money. Well I don't have your products. Boom, boom, boom!"

It was pretty funny; the fact that it happened all the time didn't slake my laughter.

Over caffeine and nicotine (I liked Susan Conyers a great deal, I realized) we talked about little things. Susan's resentment over her husband's job and their childless life oozed from every pore of the conversation. Some things were obvious, like the necessity of the "strumpet gun," but the emotional distance between them was mind-boggling. She talked about being a good FBI wife, which was easy:

"Just think about any useless appendage, and there you go."

I howled. "You have got to be kidding."

"Uh-uh. Walk softly and try not to say anything during sex. Wouldn't want to prolong it."

"Jesus. But you live in a beautiful 'burb paradise compared to the clogged excess of Lost Angeles."

"I am also independently wealthy. For me, suburbia is downward mobility." She paused to take a drag on her cigarette, paused to take in her surroundings, her neat surroundings and the steel sunshine pulsing through the windows.

"My money brought me a U.S. Gov a Mint man," she said quietly. "Best damn argument for being poor I've ever seen." And she puffed hard on that butt, puffs of exhaled smoke in her perfectly arranged living room. Is she capable of killing her child and dumping the body on Christmas morning? There are no signs of a teenager in this house, no way. Just a scent of lilacs and guilt under the cigarette smoke, guilt over having chosen existence instead of life.

Which meant that it was time for me to be a bitch. Go ahead, Jen. Cut her throat.

"I have to ask you some difficult questions, Susan."

"Sure. You said you were a private detective, right? I'm sure you didn't come all the way out here to listen to me whine." Her eyes are clear. I retrieve the photographs, stark coroner's models in black and white.

She only glances at them. "Never seen him before in my life." She hands them back.

"Are you sure?"

She wasn't nervous at all. Crime scene photos must've been part of normal dinner conversation for Fibbies; the fact that she was looking at a dead body didn't phase her at all.

"Positive."

"This teenager was found in the city subway yesterday morning. A merry Christmas present to the city. Approximately fifteen years old, white male. Killed by a lethal injection. Take another look."

"What's he, some gangbanger? He's nothing to me."

"We're not sure what he did for a living. We are relatively sure that he's your son."

One beat. Two beats. Three . . .

"And I was starting to like you, Jenny."

"DNA. One in a kazillion. Because of your husband, genetic markers for both of you are in the computer files. He's your son, but not your husband's."

Susan shook her head. "Impossible."

"DNA match to the nines. To you."

"No way."

"Susan . . ."

"No WAY!" she screamed, and stood up, straight up as if something in her chair had pushed her to her feet against her will.

"I have not had any children! What kind of fucked-up game is this? You come in, chat me up, then drop some ridiculous bombshell just to see how I react? Well I'm not playing, sister. I think you can take your coochie right back to LA where you came from."

. . . and from her mind, something darker, more interesting, the way it always is: *<it can't be that, can't be, can't be . . .>*

. . . can't be what?

Derrick is on the horn when I get back to the office. Didi is in the back, in my office, talking to one of her clients so I take the call at Didi's workstation.

"Hey, Jenny-girl. Last bit of information courtesy of LAPD's crime labs."

"Shoot."

"The drug used to kill the kid? It's an overdose of a new potion that's popular in the South Central Zone."

"What do they use it for?"

"Fuck if I know. A number of ODs show up in ERs on this side of the zone every quarter. Most survive because it's not particularly lethal unless the dose is super high."

"What is it, a hallucinogen?"

"Yeah. Cheap pharmaceutical thrills. More than that, I can't tell you."

"You got a source?"

"Not yet. But you can always go score some in the zone, if you want."

"What's your gut?"

"Dunno. Zoners might explain why the kid isn't registered anywhere."

"But a white kid? Son of an FBI agent's wife?"

"It'd be interesting to see what she says."

"Been there, done that. She says nothing. Complete denial."

"Gotta be a record of a live birth, though."

Of course. "Didi!"

From "my" office in the back: "Yeah, boss?"

"Got something for you, sweetie."

Into the phone: "Derrick? Let's do lunch one day. If you get a source on this stuff—what's it called?"

"Zombie."

Original it's not. "Zombie, lemme know."

"Sure."

Didi is standing in front of me, waiting as I hang up the phone.

"You need me, boss?"

"*Jenny,* not boss. Yeah. I need a net search. Susan Conyers, here's her social security number. We're looking for a live birth between twelve and seventeen years ago. Go city, county, state, national, international."

"You want a tiered search? I mean step it up each level if there are no hits?"

"Yup."

"Aliases?"

Hmm. Hadn't thought about that. "Maiden name and married name first. Start a parallel look for possible aliases."

"That's a big parallel, Jen. Aliases is a tough one. Does Susan Conyers have money?"

Old oil money, according to Derrick. "Yeah, she's loaded."

"Then it might be more fruitful to look for a money trail. Large transfers to a hospital, doctor, midwife from one of her sources during those time parameters."

"Okay. Start the maiden name and married name birth record search. Then look for a money trail. Then look for aliases."

"Got it." Her experience doing skip traces is going to pay off. But she's standing there looking at me.

"What?"

"You're sitting in my chair. Boss."

"Oh. Okay." Didi smiles at me and I smile back. I'm tired and I can't take another stimulant or I'll blow up. It's time to go home and try to get some sleep.

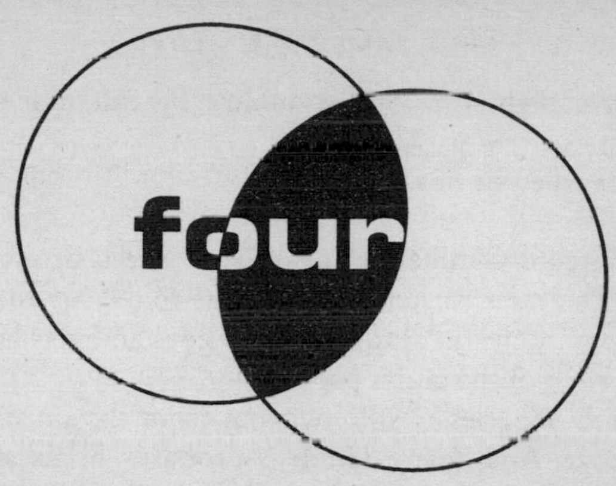

It is night in Los Angeles and he walks the streets searching. He doesn't work randomly

can't afford that

but his intended, his betrothed, is not where she's supposed to be. His power comes in knowing his victims, in finding them when they feel safe and protected, in taking them down, breaking them down, impaling them and making them accept him, their screams hiding passion amid the pain.

His impulses have quickened over the years. He seeks women more frequently, chooses targets that aren't appropriate to his calling sometimes, just to have a woman. Just to possess for a moment.

He is on a mission tonight; a woman's soft thighs are calling him, creamy white like his ejaculate, soft thighs against a hard surface, abrasive sex, power . . .

Powerful strides take him around the block of the

exclusive nightclub. She shouldn't be out alone, not tonight.

Not when he has the urge.

"Garçon! Gimme my car please." She is drunk, giggling. The valet parker makes a note to tell her that she should go home on autopilot, then goes and gets her car at the back of the club's parking lot.

Edith Wharles is still swaying from the music and the booze. And horny. Hubby's probably home asleep, certainly no thrills there. And what the hell is taking so long for my vehicle? Shit.

Her p-car is bright red, as sexy a roadster as the regulations allow. Here it comes now. Edith, my dear, must give the man a nice tip for taking forever and a day to bring it to you. There. Oops! Stupid man drove past her a little, past the entrance to the club.

Nice stupid minimum wage man opens her door. Helps her get inside. Edith fumbles in her purse for a tip, a little one for making her walk when she's fucked up—ruins the buzz.

"Here, thanks." She waves a credit bank note outside the window. But the nice stupid minimum wage man doesn't take it.

The passenger door opens. She gets a glimpse of his red valet's jacket, then a strong hand clamps over her mouth. Just screwed your tip, buddy.

"You better just drive, Edith," the stupid minimum wage man says. She doesn't like the look in his eyes. She glances down—

Sees a serpent tattoo on his arm.

Edith is going to get her thrills tonight. In spades.

* * *

It is hours later in a tacky hospital room. Edith Wharles lies on a narrow bed surrounded by monitoring equipment that is largely dormant. She is alive but heavily sedated. LAPD rape counselors and investigators have already been to see her and have taken her statement. Doctors have counseled her about getting tested for HIV infection and other venereal diseases. She sleeps heavily under the influence of drugs, a deep sleep that is mercifully dreamless. Hours pass. Bruises and muscles become sore with the passage of time. The drugs wear off. And she remembers.

And then she snaps awake. She sits bolt upright in her hospital bed, the sudden movement making her dizzy. Someone is in the room with her. A blond woman, attractive to the extent that her eyes focus.

"Who the hell are you?" she asks, thinking that she doesn't want to tell the story again.

"Jenny Sixa."

"I already talked to the police."

"I'm not LAPD."

"Then leave me alone."

"I need your help."

"My *help*? Look, I'm not in a position to help anyone right now."

He takes her to a remote area. No one is watching. Drags her out of the car, the slits in her evening dress reveal smooth thighs, delicious, she loses a heel on the rough pavement. There is a ravine by the side of the road. Early morning, there is no traffic. No one to see. He promises her he will be gentle if she doesn't resist. He doesn't want to hit her, but he will; her mouth is dry at the thought of tasting her own blood if her attacker should slap her face.

He makes her take off her clothes like they are lovers too impatient to make it home. The dress comes off, the bra, the panty hose, her underwear. The hard dirt is cold next to her white skin. He takes off his pants.

Kneels, hand over her mouth, a twisted smile as she tries to scream but screaming is pointless.

I heard her scream. The police found the nightclub's valet with a lump on his head and nothing to report. My stranger had taken him from behind, taken Edith Wharles's keys, and pulled her car around. I watched him force her to drive the car away under threat of immense bodily harm. I watched him lick his lips as her panties slid down to her ankles, felt the warm chuckle of his mind as he fell upon her.

I felt her fear as he entered her with one long fluid thrust. I felt her pain as he took her grunting and sweating for many minutes; I felt the dirt work its way into the skin on her back.

And most of all I felt her shame as he found release, the sickening wave of pleasure that a man feels when he orgasms into this useless thing, his lover, his purpose fulfilled, his power confirmed, his virility spilling onto the hard dirt in an anonymous place with a stranger he has no right to know. Not like this.

She sits on the bed with her knees drawn up to her chin, rocking softly. I don't know why I came to the hospital because talking is pointless. I can't tell her what I know, or how I know it. I can only sit with her and wait through the tears, tell her my name and let her know she's not alone.

"You've been through something like this, too, haven't you?" she asks.

I can only nod. *On a beach a long time ago in a galaxy far, far away . . .*

"I asked the police not to pursue the case. I asked them not to tell my husband."

It is a confession, *<so ashamed>* that sets her to rocking back and forth on the bed, the mask she will present to the world already forming like a scab over a soft pulpy wound in her flesh. I understand her reasoning, but it doesn't help me. Someone like Edith Wharles could get LAPD to pursue this monster by opening her checkbook and speaking the language that the cops understand. Money talks. Rapists walk, otherwise. It's an old story with a different twist because I'm a victim, too. We need a case opened just to save lover boy's DNA evidence for when we do catch him. *Shit . . .*

I have a hard time with sex, you see, and Edith, oh, Edith, seeing you dredges up too many memories.

I was nearly raped as a teenager, just as my telepathic thing had reached puberty all on its own. But there was a boy on a beach and what he wanted was more important than what I was prepared for. We both paid a heavy price for that one, and it drove my capabilities into a shell.

And it is ironic that two years later, when Mitch happened (that's what men do, they don't stay, they just occur like the weather, and then they are gone) and we talked and talked and talked, he must have sensed something about me, something . . .

And then he was gone. I remember looking up at him as he orgasmed and thinking, aha, now I'm at the peak of my power, now I'm in control, but it wasn't that at all, I'd ceased to exist.

Elvis was leaving the building and I was just another door.

He couldn't look at me afterward, like, well, I dunno.

He didn't return my phone calls.

He just disappeared. And I was hurt, I was angry. Way too angry, it turns out, way too devastated because somewhere in my head the real me was keeping score and I was oh fer two, and that just wasn't good enough.

Yet there was something about being with him, and I look at Edith and I know that maybe she'll never feel the same way about men, maybe she'll never be able to enjoy intimacy again, maybe she will always remember a dark night on a deserted road, and a man who raped her, a stranger, and I remember the last time I called Mitch, the last time I would ever call a man to inquire if he wanted to be with me again unless money was involved, lots of money for my time, thank you, and in that moment that I put the damn phone down and looked in the mirror, part of me was lost forever.

Forever.

And every day is part of that, every way that I lock myself up against getting close and deny the thoughts from strangers filling my head, *<better not to know some things, Jen>* living a long life, a long life alone with only this bastard to fill my nights with terror. It could have been so different, that one time with Mitch proved that it could be so different, but I was just a door, and he was just passing through. Well I learned my fucking lesson.

And I feel sorry that Edith has learned one, too. Sometime later I leave her my card:

Myers & Sixa
Private Investigations

and go home. Lucky me.

* * *

. . . lucky me. Lucky that he had gotten away again. He washed his face and the melancholy of what he'd done settled on him like stones, he could not look his reflection in the eye.

<*how can you stand to look at yourself*> he thought as he washed away his sweat and her perfume. He thought randomly about the way strippers looked when he'd followed them from the seedy establishments where they performed, how dressed down and depressed they looked, how they wouldn't make eye contact with anyone on the street, hair jammed under baseball caps, backpacks, dirty sneaks. He could only imagine their pain, somewhere hidden under the clothing . . .

He thought his yearning, his longing, could be described by the perfect symmetry of a woman's breast, the kind that were natural; it seemed to him in fevered moments of gazing at naked women on a stage that the real-world dressed-down dowdy types were liberated by taking off their clothes. He tried to see through their flesh into their souls, staring up at them on their pedestals, watching closely the way they discarded their skimpy clothing for clues/hints/signs . . .

In a rush he remembered trying to get Edith to take off her clothes—to ease her pain—but she was incapable of understanding, of responding on that level, incapable of understanding that his pain in taking her was far greater sacrifice than the liberation of her spirit—*yes, yes, his burden*—he was the only one who understood the dynamics of his hurt and that of his *victims.*

If you could honestly call them that.

And when he gazed at strippers on a stage, undulating slowly to music, what exactly was he seeking? What did he want? What did they want? Was it the money crumpled up and tossed at their feet? He didn't think so. He knew they mostly hated the men and would just as soon spit on the money . . .

You could see the distance in the pretty ones as they undulated slowly under dark red lights on tattered stages cracked with age, as they danced in front of men too stupid to see the depths within them even as they stared at their lovely bodies, bodies that he knew had been caressed in ways that did harm, loved in ways that left scars. They left these places dressed down, hidden, and revealed themselves only to men who were too scared to touch them. He was not afraid when he took women, as he loved them, as he liberated them . . .

What did he want? Was it sex? Is that what he wanted? He'd tried prostitutes, amazed at the mechanical aspects of it, like they were lubricated with oil, like money was greasing the wheels, while they casually smoked cigarettes as he grunted astride them searching for release that simply wasn't there. Prostitutes had no appreciation for his self-sacrifice in liberating them from their clothing, from their veils, from their hidden selves.

He looked at himself in the mirror, this strange face, full of fear, full of awful knowledge

*<you **raped** her you fool>*

that he had achieved release inside Edith Wharles and plunged to the very bottom of his sins

<extremism in the pursuit of perfection is no sin>

and at the very bottom, as always, there was but one way out as he slapped the light switch in his quarters—***why do you persist?***

<moderation in the pursuit of purity is no virtue>
and went to the door of the equipment room, carefully logging in, undoing the sealed hatches, gazed at the padded couch under the long banks of bluish fluorescent lights, listened to the computers softly humming, off-line.

<but you raped her . . .>
Frantic, he strapped himself into the padded couch, one hand already on the console keyboard running sequences, powering up, the other strapping on the headgear and the electrodes and the monitoring outputs.

<you are addicted . . .>
His fear drove him through the checklists very quickly, as always, and he did not, could not relax until the computers had taken over.

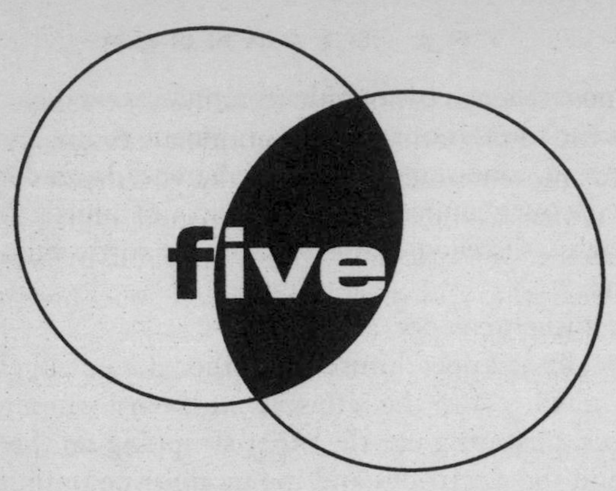

A remedy is what I'm seeking. By the next day I need to get out and get some action. Didi is against it, but I'm in need of risk. Derrick says Zombie is a new drug of choice in the South Central Zone so here we go to grandmother's house. Chasing a kid killer and packing a gun might wash the taste of Edith Wharles out of my system.

What used to be South Central Los Angeles was barricaded off in the early part of the twenty-first century. A number of urban crime zones were designated during that period as the last gasp of out-of-control society to control the urban underclass. The ethnic urban middle and upper classes were powerless to stop what amounted to massive segregation enforced by National Guard troops with orders to shoot to kill anyone trying to exit the zone without proper papers. Some even agreed with this supposed "final response" to crime.

It didn't make the problems go away. It legitimized a thousand years of race hatred and brought it out into the open. It was fashionable to talk about zoners as the root of all evil; dark skin, an entitlements card, and no job was more than enough to make you the devil incarnate. Worse, though, was that it created a huge area for criminals to operate in without restraint in every city that tried the approach; there were unconfirmed reports, like UFO sightings, that Colombians had huge airfields devoted to receiving contraband secreted in the Harlem, New York City, crime zone.

And contrary to popular belief, the zones were not freestyle prisons. Nope, still needed plenty of them and we couldn't seem to build them fast enough. And why not?

The legitimate world required more and more advantages in order to make it. Even if you did everything right, making it was not guaranteed. The underworld took people on a "come as you are" basis just as the legitimate world told people "don't come if you aren't . . ." If you aren't white, aren't educated, if you don't have skills, if you don't have money, if you won't move to Taiwan to build subassemblies for pennies a day, if your school sucks, if your parents didn't love you enough . . . think you got problems, sister? Screw you. Next in line. The zones were the worst of the massive ghettoization of American culture, but the elderly, the down on their luck, the infirm, needed ghettos, too. They just weren't guarded by troops with guns. If you were white, or were lucky enough to be born outside of the zone, you could suffer poverty with more of your rights intact, but you would still suffer. You would suffer bad. And if you were rich you could build yourself a hacienda guarded by thuggish-looking gentlemen with submachine guns and look the other way. Maybe even chopper to your neighbor's hacienda so your feet didn't have to touch the disease-ridden ground.

The checkpoint is manned by bored troops in khaki camouflage fatigues. I catch one errant thought—*<must be lookin' to be fuckbait>*—that suggests that white troops don't think much of me going into the zone by myself. (Yet another myth about the zone—entrance by whites = **Instant Death**. What hooey.) The black troops don't think about me, try not to think about anything much, it seems, and especially don't think about shooting other black people trying to bust the zone.

The barricade is heavily fortified and scarred with bullet holes. Two years ago there was a major disturbance in the zone, riots that took heavy measures to quell. The soldier looking at my ID waves laconically to his counterpart at the barrier, and the entrance to the South Central Zone slowly raises.

Am I sure I want to do this?

The grunt at the barrier waves me through thinking, *<better go if you're goin'>*

Yeah, Gomer. Better go if I'm going.

Urban society after the apocalypse: There are no services anymore, no electricity, water and sewer shaky, phone lines only to the extent that you could tap an old trunk line that the central office forgot to reroute. People still work outside of the zone at marginal jobs that allow them to keep food on the table. Entrepreneurs still service the indigenous population at prices Arab oil sheikhs would have trouble paying. Internal combustion still rules the zone even though gasoline is scarce. Cars are scarce, traffic consists of masses of people walking through the streets with their heads down, the living dead. The buildings are dying, consumed by fire, pockmarked with heavy caliber impacts.

There are plots of land everywhere, embarrassing green in the midst of urban decay. Vegetables. Chicken coops. The population has thinned to that which can be supported by marginal employment outside the zone, entrepreneurship, and the underground.

Oh, yes. The underground. Whole blocks of turf marked with colors and blocked by angry young men with pump guns. Open-air drug marketplaces to soak up some of the cash that floats in over the barriers. Gunshots and firecrackers. The faces of nightmares. Ragtag kids playing, smiling, resilient.

One mean little hombre stops me, holds up his hand in front of my p-car. He's wearing a diagonal white belt, like a patrol boy charged with helping his peers cross the street at school. He's also wearing bandoliers criss-crossing his chest and two shoulder holsters that are knotted so they don't hang down to his ankles. The bandoliers are empty of shells, the holsters have two pistols in them. One of the guns is a six-shooter cap pistol, a kid's toy. The other looks like an ancient Glock nine-millimeter.

Hombre saunters up to my window with a smile on his face like a local traffic cop trying to assist a lost motorist. I roll down my window letting in the stench of rotting garbage and smoke.

"Hold up, white lady. You look mighty lost."

"I'm looking for something."

Broad grin. "Drugs? Black magic sex?"

"Drugs."

"Oh. My name's Richie." He sticks his hand through the window.

"Jenny." I shake his tiny hand. Richie can't be more than ten.

"I'm not the guy to see about some drugs, white lady. I'm just waiting for my brother. Maybe he can help you."

"Will he be back soon?"

"Him? Oh, sure." In a smooth motion he pulls the Glock from its holster, holds it upright, and ejects the clip. Shows it to me.

"See? No bullets. One in the chamber. Hurt some mudderfucker really bad if somethin' happens, then I'm s'posed to run away."

"Uh, okay." He looks at me like I'm stupid, like I don't get it.

"My brother wouldn't leave me with no bullets if he was goin' be long," Richie explains.

I park the car and wait with Richie for his brother. Half a block away is an area marked with white rags tied to sticks in the ground. I ask Richie what it means.

"Ol' people. Sick people. The flags mean 'keep away.' "

"Oh." There must be two acres of sick people. The wind shifts and I can smell the bodies, the excretions, the blood- and puss-soaked wrappings and bandages, the corruption.

The death.

"Can I ask you something?"

"Sure."

"You don't look like a junkie."

"I'm not."

"You look kinda rich."

"I am." *Bad thing to admit to in the zone, Jen.*

"Then why you here?"

"I need to find a particular drug. But it's not for me."

"Who's it for?"

"No one, really. I'm trying to figure something out."

"Yeah? What?"

Kids . . . "Somebody I know died from this drug. I want to find out where it came from."

"People die alla time, white lady. They do drugs, or they get sick, somebody kilts them. Alla time."

"My friend died outside the zone."

"Does that make it special?"

"To me it does."

He considers this.

"Was he white like you?"

"Yes."

"That's what makes it special, huh."

I say nothing to that. There's nothing I can say.

"Lady, you think I'm a thief?"

"No, Richie."

"Then why am I in here and you out there bein' rich?"

"I . . . don't know, Richie."

"I think somebody stole the future. Long time ago." He takes the Glock out of its holster, plays with it like it was a six-shooter.

"It wasn't me, Richie."

"Didn't say *that*. My brother says if somebody steals something good, like food, and you eat some of it, it's not the same as stealing."

"Why's that?"

"It's just *tastin'*. Difference is that it's already stole, and it ain't going back. Why not get a taste?"

"And what do you say about that?"

Richie the philosopher looks at me sideways and sardonic. "I think you got a *taste*, white lady. Big time."

Big brother is a gangly teenager, maybe as old as John Doe 2. He gawks at his little bro's "white lady."

"Whatever you want, I ain't got it."

"Information. I can pay."

"Maybe we don't want your money."

"I just have one question. Thousand bucks."

"Show me the money."

I'd yanked a bill out of my purse when Richie stopped me. I hold it out like it's the last money in this universe.

Big bro shakes his head. "Looks like a lot, but I want no part of whatever you're messin' with."

"Just hear me out. Where can I get some Zombie?"

It got so quiet you'd have thought a fucking neutron bomb had gone off and killed all the people. Their faces were like stone and whatever knowledge they had about Zombie was the chisel.

"C'mon, Richie. We gotta go." Big bro takes the youngster's hand. Richie looks like he's going to cry, his face and cheeks twisted up.

"Wait." But big bro is angry now, shakes me off, Richie starts to cry.

"Gimme my bullets, Joe-l! We gonna die, ain't we?" he wails.

<shut up> Joel thinks and Richie wails:

<you did it. you stole the future>

<You Did It> and a final thought from Joel:

<just wait here—you'll get your Zombies> as he drags the little one away.

* * *

Day fades into night in the zone. I stand and lean against my p-car, gun drawn, cocked, and locked. Spare magazines in easy reach. Zombie hunting. Waiting.

Strange, people of color served in every war, in every profession, in all walks of life. The core of our embrace to them—the barbed wire of the plantation, the barrel of a gun, the end of a nightstick, an electrified perimeter guarded by men instructed to kill. Fear. Loathing. Envy. I am not tripping the white guilt trip here, I am not singing old Negro spirituals. I make no excuses for who they are, what some of them do, have done, will do. I am feeling what we did, what we didn't do, and taking responsibility for that, turning it in my head, knowing that from the warmth of a mutual embrace we both would have been infinitely better off.

There is a sound, like the shuffling of many tired feet in the distance and a sigh from somewhere near the old sick people's encampment. Something is coming.

I consider turning the headlights of the p-car on and shining them down the road, but I think better of drawing attention to myself. A whistle, a rustle, garb shifting around dusty ankles and legs, many of them, and it goes to the core of my white fear in the heart of blackness. Chanting, eerie echoes off blasted walls ravaged by fire, words unexplained. I can see them, perhaps twenty men and women, heads bowed, shuffling through the street, moving toward the old people's compound. A slight sigh of dry wind pushes the white rags marking their area.

I can make out individuals now. Eyes fixed in their heads, they do not blink. Legs moving in unison, they do not deviate. As they turn into the old people's compound, a young girl runs away from their march screaming. Against all will I move closer.

And closer still. Whoever they are wouldn't hardly notice me, it seems, even if I joined the procession. The old people's camp is open ground filled with beds, no shelter from the elements or the smog because it rarely rains in southern California. Men and women, some young, most old, lay on thin cots jammed together, only the occasional cough or movement of a limb indicates that any are alive. The crowd, the zombies, have gathered around one old woman's bed.

"Come on, old mother," the leader, a tall gaunt man with a wisp of beard, says to the immobile body on the cot. He is carrying a canteen. Two helpers lift the old woman's head and shoulders from the mattress; she is stiff and doesn't bend at the waist.

Stiff. As in rigor mortis? There is little thought coming from the entire group except the leader and his thoughts are a jumble—

<lifeo fcrow na thee giv ewilli andde athunto faithful thoub edays ten tribulation . . .>

"Come on, old mother." The leader pours some of the canteen into her lifeless mouth. Most of it dribbles down her smock creating a darkening stain.

<suffers halt thou whicht hings thoseo fnonefear>

"Come on, OLD MOTHER!" the leader cries, and slaps the corpse forward and back, the blows dull against dead flesh—

<lifeof treeth eof eatto giveiw ill overcomethth athimto>

"COME ON, OLD MOTHER!" he screams, a final insult, a final blow—

<old mother is awake!>

The thought is a jolt to me, electric like a signal hitting speakers with the volume turned up full, and she coughs as she thinks this, sputtering liquid in a hoarse cloud. Old mother swings her hips slowly, painfully from the cot, stands like the walking dead, and joins her place in the procession.

"Old mother is reborn! Hallelujah," the leader says softly.

Begins to walk away from the sick place, shuffling with the weight of death seemingly on their shoulders.

"The truth," old mother whispers and the leader says four words:

"Wu, ting, fill, wela."

Old mother repeats the sounds . . .

I wade into the crowd, parting it like the Red Sea. They do not see me, they do not touch me. They do not know I even exist. Old mother is in the rear, walking next to the leader. My gun hand held high over my head, I thread through until I am next to her and reach out to touch her hand.

Her flesh has the chill of death. Her mind, her last thoughts . . .

<The passwords to heaven>

And old mother grabs my hand and stares at me, her mind a vortex sucking me down, old mother's grip like iron, the thought *<whore>* her eyes wide as she stares through me as if she can see everything I am and I can see everything that she has come through, the stench of death in her mind . . .

I black out.

"White lady? White lady, wake up!"

A little boy's hand shakes me senseless. Knowledge comes back slowly alongside awareness. Where I am. Why. What I saw. *The truth . . . the passwords to heaven?*

"Are you okay?" Richie of the twin guns is standing over me looking concerned.

"Um, I think. How long have I been out?"

"Five minutes. Maybe less."

Then the zombies aren't that far away. In fact I can hear their shuffle and someone's wail of "Old mother!" in the distance.

"I thought they kilt you."

"No."

"Then you better go."

"Why? They never even noticed me."

Richie shakes his head. "They notice everything."

Words I didn't understand. "Richie, do you know what . . ."

The rifle shot stiffens the boy as the impact digs out a puff of dirt between us. Somebody shooting and my reaction is automatic—

"Run!"

I scramble to my feet and haul the little hombre to his. It's half a block to the safety of my p-car. More shots, the echo makes it hard to tell where they're coming from. Crouching low, we run toward the car.

chunka-chunka-chunka . . . a weapon on full automatic chews up the ground in front of us. No choice now but to stand and fight . . .

. . . and an icy fear grips my bowels at the thought of trading shots with old mother holding an Uzi and a stone-cold face, my bullets ripping away chunks of her with no effect, impossible to kill already dead flesh . . .

Richie wheels around, the ancient Glock in hand, and snaps off three quick rounds. I still can't see muzzle flash from our attacker, my own shots are more tentative.

Chunka-chunka-chunka . . . there! Fuck (three rounds right above the muzzle flash) you!

Then the second gun opens up.

"Damn, Richie, we have to give up!" Less than a quarter of a block from my car. Damn!

"No way! No way!"

"Richie, listen to me! It's a crossfire. Stop shooting! Lay your gun down!"

I put my pistol in the dirt. Push hombre's hand down so that he stops shooting.

"Put the gun down, Richie."

I stand back up, hands in the air as Richie kneels to place his pistol in the dirt. The hostiles have stopped shooting and are walking toward us.

Shuffling. Heads down. Guns gripped awkwardly in curled wasted limbs. Dead men are walking toward us.

Gunshots begin again in rapid succession, good solid hits in their torsos *having no effect* . . .

"Go for the heads!" I scream.

Blam! The right one's cranium explodes and he drops to a knee. *Blam, blam!*

The second one goes down.

Richie yells, "I got 'em! I got 'em!" and I look down and see his toy cap pistol lying in the dirt beside my gun, his ancient Glock smoking in his hand.

Richie and I part company ("You didn't say which gun, white lady . . .") and I put the p-car's defensive systems on full alert. I scream through the South Central Zone with my car yelling in monotone "Don't fuck with the car, don't fuck with the car, I will hurt you" through its external speaker. As I pass through the barrier I shudder as I remember touching old mother's hand and slipping inside her mind.

I can't describe it, I can't explain it. But what's in old mother's mind is the experience of death itself, death and, somehow, something else, and I am feeling the hollow core of my life, empty and desperate, the very opposite of the remedy that I was seeking, another mystery wrapped in an enigma.

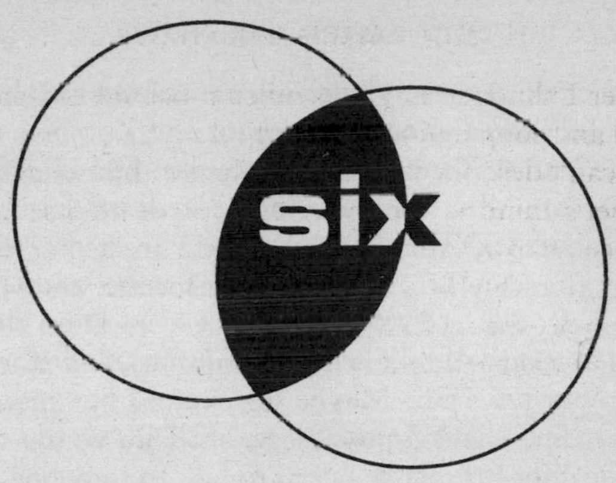

I can't go home and sleep, no way. I go to the office. Didi has mercifully gone home so I can be alone, truly.

I go to my desk and start to diagram the case. Really cases. We have a drug common to zoners and white teenage dead boys. One circle. We have a serial rapist. Another circle. We have Susan Conyers who denies having a son that turned up dead. She goes into the first circle. We have Edith Wharles who was raped. Second circle. Gotta check with Didi on the results of her search for a live birth record for Susan Conyers. I wish I could simply go back to being rich.

Didi has left me a message slip since she knows I don't check my electronic gizmos for such things. Mitch Belford called, wanting to have lunch. Yeah, sure. Screw lunch. I can't even remember the last time I had something to eat. Maybe that's your stomach grumbling now, Jenny.

I yawn heavily, bad move. Don't want to go to sleep. Not yet. I have to figure out what to do about the second circle because it's driving me crazy. I also have to figure out who I should tell about the Zombies in the South Central Zone. Derrick? Nope. LAPD officially doesn't care what happens in the zone and is unofficially racist. Like we all are.

My friends? Hah. Betty wouldn't understand. None of them would understand. It's not a question that revolves around self, like where to summer this year.

I could tell Didi. Maybe go over to her place and chat her up. That's a possibility, but Didi would be too analytical for my tastes. I need to talk to someone about the emotional side of what's going on. I briefly think of Edith Wharles, or Susan Conyers, but neither is a convincing choice because the payoff for me emotionally is too uncertain.

I must've been dozing when the phone rang, chimed, actually. I automatically fumbled the receiver from its cradle without thinking. It's an audio only call—my wall doesn't light up with the caller's picture.

"Hello?" I glance at my watch. One in the morning.

"Jenny? Jenny Sixa?"

"Uh, yeah. Who's this?"

"Mitch. Mitch Belford. From the party. From the past."

Like I want to reminisce with this bastard right now . . . "Yeah, I remember. Didi said you'd called. About lunch."

"Yes, yes I did. I called about lunch. Can we?"

"Well it's a little late in the evening to be making social plans, Mitch. And if you're trying to rekindle old flames, well, I just dunno if it's a good idea . . ." *Not to mention half a very fucked-up lifetime too late* . . .

"Why do you think I called you at one in the morning?"

"I, er, have no idea."

"Because I was thinking about you."

"Um, listen, Mitch, high school was a long time ago."

He snorts into the phone. "This isn't about romance, Jenny."

As *if* . . . "Oh. Then what is this about, Mitch?"

"I got a strong feeling at the party that you need someone to talk to."

I'm the telepath, here, pal. "How's that?"

"I used to be a priest, Jenny. I haven't been out of the order so long that I don't retain some pastoral skills. Like knowing when people are troubled."

I'm reminded of the confidence game gimmick, the essence of which is find someone who's lonely and talk them out of their money. "I'm a wealthy socialite in Los Angeles, Mitch. Why do you think I'm troubled?"

"Precisely because you're a wealthy socialite in Los Angeles. That and something in your eyes, I think."

"So you sit up nights thinking about poor rich women you banged once?"

His chuckle is part shudder, it seems. "That's too short a list to keep me awake at nights. I'm simply offering a trade. I'll tell you what bothers me if you'll tell me what bothers you. Deal?"

Not that I'm going to tell him anything significant, but the little things . . .

"Fine, whatever. How about today?"

"This afternoon? Sure. I can even suggest a place."

And he does.

That afternoon, after a most comfortable dreamless snooze curled up at my desk I meet Mitch Belford at some honky-tonk joint not ten blocks from the barrier to the South Central Zone. Man, even the p-car was nervous about being this close.

Mitch has the kind of open expression on his face that one associates with confession. Forgive me, father, for I have sinned, that kind of stuff. He takes my hand warmly but not sexually, and we sit on a terrace overlooking the street. *He never returned my calls . . .*

"It's true, isn't it? You're a capable?"

Capable, as in capable of reading people's thoughts. "Yes, it's true."

"You weren't a telepath . . . when we . . ."

I was but I didn't know it. Otherwise we wouldn't have . . . "I'd repressed a lot of things, y'know, bad things . . . we happened because I thought . . . I was confused . . . and you were there." *And then you weren't . . .*

"In a bizarre sort of way, I guess I was. I think I was searching, too." He turns away for a moment not wishing to relive . . . the memories . . .

"So the listing for your agency isn't hype."

"Nope. Why do you ask?"

"Because my vows prevent me from revealing what I've learned from confession even after I've left the order. I therefore protected myself from your talents."

Masque. It prevents me from reading a normal person's thoughts.

I shrug, but there's an electric shock to this. He and I were *intimate* by choice once upon a time. Now he needs to protect himself from me because I'm a telepath, my cursed talent, my sin seals all of that past away. *Of all people . . . now he's just a stranger, too.*

"So. Who should talk first? Me or you, Jenny?"

That's easy. "You."

"Fine. Hopefully I won't bore you." He sips his water for a second, then continues—

"I'd decided on the priesthood relatively late in life, when I was in my mid-twenties."

"Why is that considered late?"

"Because most who have the calling have it relatively early and don't dabble in worldly things the way that I did."

Well, Jenny, score one for being a worldly thang. "You mean like you and I."

He blushes a bit. "Yes. Like you and I."

It was so intense, like we'd fused .. he asked me if I was a virgin and I lied without thinking about it because I needed to be . . .

"Were there others, Mitch?" *. . . and I always thought he knew I was lying, maybe I told him about the other time, on the beach, maybe he knew almost two decades before I would admit it to myself . . . the secrets we tell strangers, and how we tell them . . .*

"No, oh, no. That was one of the ways I knew I had a calling. One of the things that told me that I was certainly of the world, but not quite in it."

Join the club. "But the priesthood?" Running away was so noble, Mitch. *Men . . .*

"I was literally consumed with faith, Jenny. I wanted nothing more than to understand religion and understand God. Sex didn't fulfill me; celibacy seemed more natural. My religiosity filled me up and kept me full."

"So why Church of the Resurrection?"

"Somewhat more progressive than Catholicism. Smaller, less steeped in tradition. And I thought less political."

"Less political than what?"

"Any large organization has internal politics, Jenny. The Catholic church is rife with internal factions. Every new pope brings in his own people and thinking. True, there isn't much deviance in the doctrinal basis for the faith, but there is wide latitude for interpreting Scripture and other authoritative sources to assist us in today's world."

"So why did you leave?"

He looks out over the terrace at the traffic passing by. "Lots of reasons. Quite good ones, actually. The church . . ."

"I was talking about me, Mitch. Not your job."

He looks away, distant for a moment, a moment in time that we lost forever.

"I . . . it wasn't right. It just wasn't right."

"For you, maybe. What about me?"

"My faith was my life, Jenny. The church was my life. Something about that night crystallized it in my head, and that's all I could think of."

"Are you still a believer?" *Was walking away worth it?*

He sighs. "Somewhat. I just can't deny our wretched existence. To me that confounds faith, flies in the face of what I am supposed to believe about God. The things I've heard in confession . . ."

"Do you ever attend church services?"

His voice drops to a whisper. "No. Rarely."

He looks at me as a signal to stop for a moment.

"Let's start with you, Jenny. If you don't mind."

"Okay. I'm a telepath, quite powerful. I hear a constant babble of thoughts around me unless I take drugs to dull my senses. I'm also quite rich. Inherited a huge sum of money based upon a case I solved two years ago."

"The Waters Industries investigation."

"Very good. It was all so hushed up not many people know that I was involved."

"And now you hide your abilities behind drugs."

"Yes."

"Even though you probably have a unique ability to help people with their deepest fears and troubles. Even though you could counsel youth more effectively than any guidance counselor in any school, for example."

"Wait a sec. What makes you think I could do any of that?"

"Because as a telepath, you are instantly closer to people's inner thoughts than any normal could ever be. People couldn't lie to you, Jenny. People couldn't hide behind words or denial. You could really connect with someone quickly and really bring them out of their shell."

"But I try to avoid casual contact."

"Casual contact, sure. But if you knew how many times I wished I had even a tiny fraction of your abilities as a priest in confession, just to be able to reach out and know someone's guilt and ease their pain, you'd see your talents in a new light."

Would I? I've peered into enough dead people's minds; I've heard enough filth from the living to seriously dispute that statement.

"Besides, what made you choose such a dark path for using your talents? What made you get involved with crimes and criminals?"

"Is that important?"

"Of course it is. We all seek completion in others, in strangers. The special person we grow to love and marry. The child that develops into an independent person. Why have you sought completion in victims? Dead victims at that?"

Why indeed? "The past." And you, my fine feathered friend, are part of that past.

"But there can't be any satisfaction in connecting with the dead. Their problems simply become your own because you're the only one left who can do something about them."

"But I can't change my past." *I can't take back that one moment of intimacy, can't stand to be used and left alone . . .*

"No need to. What you need to think about is changing your future."

"How?"

"Depends. I'm going to give you something to read, then we can talk about it, okay? This monograph won't have all the answers or any answers, but it's a beginning."

"Okay." I try and hide my skepticism.

Lunch comes and we eat. It is quite good, actually, and cheap.

"So, I've really enjoyed your company today, Jenny."

I must admit it's been fun. I mean after the angst and all. I've actually forgotten about my life for a few precious moments.

"I promised you a monograph." He pulls two, no, three sheets of paper from his bag and hands them to me.

"So this is the key to spiritual enlightenment?"

Mitch laughs. "There isn't a single key to spiritual enlightenment."

"Then why would someone like you leave the priesthood? Why did you lose your faith?"

He looks off into the distance, focused not on the buildings across the noisy street, but something much farther away. "I lost faith with two thousand plus years of mumbo jumbo that may or may not have any basis in reality. If there is a God, let Him show Himself. Let Him be more than a two-thousand-year-old myth."

He looks at me. "Do you believe in miracles, Jenny?"

I shrug. "Not really."

"Neither do I. I can't find it in my heart to believe that He is coming back. It would be a miracle for Him to walk this earth again. We simply aren't worthy. I'm simply not worthy. I couldn't go on using the power of God's name to pass judgment on people. Not without some renewal, some sign . . ."

He starts to say something else, but then I get slammed with a broadcast of thoughts so strong that I think that my rapist friend from my nightmares must be sitting next to me. I actually choke on the water that I was sipping, but Mitch doesn't notice—*he's staring wide-eyed at something behind me*—

<suffers halt thou whicht hings thoseo fnonefear>

"Get down!" I scream as the automatic weapon opens up.

"Everyone get down!" *Chunka-chunka-chunka* . . . I leap over the table and slam Mitch over backward in his chair. "Stay down!" I whisper to him as fiercely as I can. And then I reach into my purse and pull out my gun.

<you heard the Truth> he thinks as bits of china and glass fly everywhere as his bullets scour the terrace. I can't see the gunman; all I see is other diners on their knees screaming and weeping and scrambling

to get clear. The message, <*old mother wants to see you!*> is overpowering . . .

I see it from his view, now. Waitress rushes through the glass doors leading inside the restaurant and he cuts her down, the throbbing gun barely felt against his deadened arms. He sweeps the terrace again, finger firmly pressed against the trigger and the AK-47 set to full auto. He jams in another clip and walks forward, ignoring the diners huddled on the floor crying . . .

He's looking for me.

I struggle to remember the layout of the terrace so that I can juxtapose him in my mind. I'm going to jump up and take him out. Are we cocked and locked, Jenny?

Yes. Pray you aren't facing the wrong direction when you stand up.

Wait. I sneak a peek. Yes, there he is over there. Tall thin black man in rags, moving like he's been dead a hundred years. Automatic weapon. Full clip.

I haven't been shooting much in the last two years. And if last night in the zone was any indication, you're flaking rust.

You had skills, girlfriend. Use 'em or lose 'em.

But he turns toward me as I stand up, and our fingers depress the triggers at about the same time.

Derrick Trent has an army of police officers at the restaurant as a show of force this close to the South Central Zone. Mitch is okay, I'm okay. The only fatality was the waitress who came running onto the terrace in the middle of the firefight.

And the zoner souped up on Zombie.

"So how do you think he got out of the zone?" I ask Trent.

"No way that's legitimate. This man had no papers and was definitely not cleared to exit the zone under any circumstances."

"But it happens all the time, doesn't it?"

"What? Oh, sure. Money creates opportunities to bust the containment. No doubt about it."

"Hmm."

"Now you say he was looking for you?"

"Seemed like it."

"What'd you pick up from his head?"

"Gibberish. Similar to what I heard in the zone yesterday." *Why would old mother want me?*

"Yesterday? You went to South Central yesterday?"

I pull him aside. "I was looking for Zombie." And found something the corpse thought was "The Truth."

"Oh. I take it you found it."

"I'll say. And look what came back to find me."

"But how could he know that you were this close to the zone?"

A chilling thought. What if it was irrelevant where I was? What if there's an army of creeps roaming the streets searching for me?

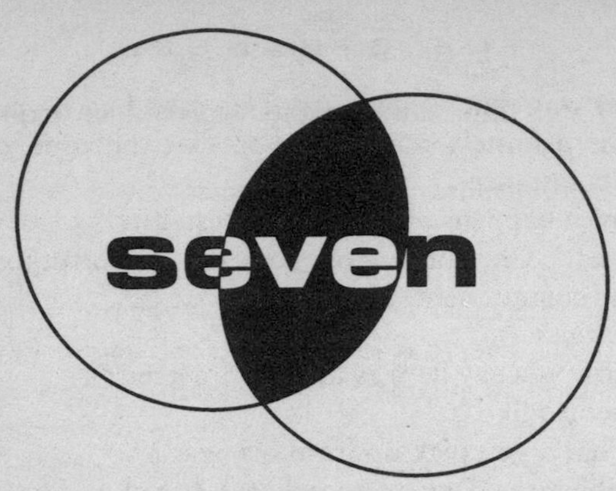

Christ, dead zoners chasing me in the real world. Man, Didi, I need answers, and I need 'em fast. I hustle back to the office with Mitch Belford in tow, all sins of the past forgotten for uno momento.

"Deeds, gimme a sitrep on what's been going on."

"Sure. Conyers search and destroy mission. Screened seventeen trillion transactions so far, no hits on either her married or maiden name. Software agents are now looking internationally for transactions that match the parameters."

"A big zero. Okay, I need you to debrief me on what happened in the zone and today at lunch. Okay?"

"Sure. Hi," Didi says to Mitch, "I'm Deeds."

"Pleased to meet you, Deeds."

It occurs to me that Mitch doesn't have a clue as to what we're working on.

So I begin talking.

* * *

As I shift into the thoughts I picked up from the zoners Mitch stops me.

"Can you transcribe it more exactly?"

"Why?"

"Because it's a puzzle. It may be another language. But we need as exact a transcription as you can provide."

"Hmm." Everyone carries microprocessors buried in their necks to augment their mental processes. Some, like me, digitize everything on a twenty-four-hour loop so that I can reconstruct what's happened to me up to twenty-four hours ago. All I have to do is get it out.

"I need a processor to processor shunt, Deeds."

"You dumping or accessing?"

"I'm dumping the twenty-four-hour file so we can try and translate the thoughts I picked up from the Zombies."

The word "Zombies" stops Mitch. "What did you call them?"

"Zombies. These people appear to use a peculiar hallucinogen called Zombie. It originates in the zone."

He struggles with something, like the term "Zombies" has a special meaning for him. It's a shame he's on Masque because I would simply read him like an open book. In the end he says nothing.

"Deeds? You ready?"

She has two slender gold-impregnated cables leading from her workstation and waiting to be plugged into the sockets at the base of my neck.

"Ready, boss."

"Let her rip."

It takes Didi some time to edit down the file to the point where I encounter the Zombies in the zone.

In the end there are three separate passages of gibberish:

1. *lifeo fcrow na thee giv ewilli andde athunto faithful thoub edays ten tribulation.*

2. *suffers halt thou whicht hings thoseo fnonefear.*

3. *lifeof treeth eof eatto giveiw ill overcomethth athimto.*

But the processors crap out on the four Hindustan sounding words. No translation possible.

"What did they say about this?" Didi asks.

"They called it the Truth. The old woman thought they were the passwords to heaven."

"What do you think, Mitch?" Didi asks. He's looking at the three garbled phrases.

"The first three look like English with some of the words scrambled a bit. See the word 'Suffers' in passage two and 'thee' in passage one. Wait a second—"

He takes a pad and scribbles for a moment. "Look, in passage three the words 'life, of, tree' are all run together. I bet if we simply play with this we'll get English words from all of it."

"And what about the other part? The four words?"

"I could downlink a Hindustan phonetics processor," Didi says helpfully.

"That's assuming they're Hindustani. Let's concentrate on what we have because I think we can crack that. The rest?" He shrugs. "I wouldn't worry about it. There's no such thing as a password to heaven."

Didi begins noodling the passages to break out as many English language words as she can. Mitch is rubbing his forehead like something's bothering him.

"Something wrong?"

"I'm not sure. The words are consistent with scripture of some kind. 'Thee.' 'Suffers.' " He looks at me. "I wouldn't be surprised if this is a passage from the Bible or some other religious text."

"Hmm. Then what would that mean?"

"I don't know. How confident are we of the algorithm?"

This is Didi's department. She used a phonetics program to provide an exact translation of my memories.

"Confidence is high, boss."

Some minutes later Derrick Trent calls in looking for me.

"Yeah, Derrick."

"I need you, Jenny."

Alarms go off in my gut. "What . . . happened?"

"A third John Doe. White male. Looks about fifteen, same as the others. No ID, nothing in the net."

"How long ago?"

"He's fresh. I've instructed them to pack the body in ice and wait for you. Chopper's in the air now heading for the helipad on your roof."

"How did he die?"

"Same as the others."

My stomach flops over. Zoners and dead white kids. What in the world is going on?

"On my way, Derrick."

I tell Didi and Mitch to continue looking at the gibberish while I'm gone.

They found the body on the beach at Santa Monica. Santa Monica PD called it in when they found it fit the profile of cases that LAPD was interested in. The helicopter sets me down in a parking lot a short walk from where they found the body. John Doe 3 is zipped into a body bag filled with ice. SMPD followed the instructions to the letter and there will be a great deal for me to connect with.

The thought does not give me much comfort.

Derrick stands waiting, hands on his hips, suit jacket flapping in the gentle onshore breeze.

"Was he killed here?" I ask him, knowing that's what he wants me to ask him.

"Possibly. Or they may have shot him up elsewhere and brought him here to OD by himself." Derrick shrugs.

I shiver. Bad feelings, bad bad feelings. I fucking hate beaches anyway. It's a personal thing.

They unzip the body bag. John Doe 3 is white, fifteen or thereabouts, with a shaved head. Nondescript clothing. Remembering the other bodies, I check his right hand and left foot for puncture wounds that are not involved with the cause of death. While John Doe 3 does not have wounds in either of these places, there is a clean, bloodless puncture wound on his left hand. I make a mental note to have LAPD look closely at the wounds, but of course I'm only trying to postpone the inevitable. *I went to a garden party . . .*

I kneel down in the sand, then lay in the sand next to the body.

. . . to reminisce with my old friends . . . Carefully I touch his face.

It is cold, damp. A cavern of sorts. Candles, hundreds of them. John Doe 3 is seated at a low table filled with plain food. Across from him sits another boy, also white, also about the same age. There is the rustle of a robe nearby but 3 doesn't turn to look. I sense a strong need to be obedient to his captives.

The robes are hooded, obscuring faces. They are

gathering around the other boy; JD 3 studies him carefully. One of them stands aside, a guard with an ugly weapon, an automatic rifle.

The other (John Doe #??) nods in 3's direction as the robes gather around him. John Doe 3 watches calmly as if he's seen this all before.

The robes are doing something to the other boy. Wrapping something around his face, his head.

The robes step clear and an odd detail jumps out—at least two of them are wearing holsters around their waists that look like they contain guns. But John 3 is focused on the other boy—they've wrapped the other boy's head in some kind of headgear that leaves openings only for his nose. The robes help him to his feet as he shakes his head to get the helmet to sit comfortably. John 3 watches as John 4 is taken away, noticing for an instant the fittings on the helmet, electrodes, studs, receptacle plugs. There is a room down the hall that John Doe 4 is led to and a heavy door that they unlatch. As the group enters the room beyond lights come on but there isn't any detail that suggests the room's form or purpose.

Then one of them begins pointing at John Doe 3 and shouting, there's a commotion like a mistake has been made.

The robes descend upon John Doe 3, and he feels a pinprick in his neck.

Then the world begins spinning . . .

I resurface at that point, not wanting to ride all the way down with the young victim. I am gasping for breath—the memory of old mother and the absolute heart of darkness in her head haunts me.

I can't stop coughing. Derrick hugs me, crushes me to him.

"It's okay, Jen. S'okay."

But it's not okay. John Doe 3 was standing at the edge of the same precipice as old mother in the zone, sliding toward the great cold void that old mother had already traversed and come out on the other side.

"What'd you see?" Derrick asks me gently.

"A lot. Too much. Bunch of religious nuts or something, a cavern with lots of candles. No faces, though, nothing tangible. They had guns, some of them."

"Anything else?"

"Yeah. Quite possibly I saw John Doe 4."

"Was he . . ."

"Yes. About the same age. Shaved head. White." I pause long enough to shiver.

"Where are they getting these kids, Derrick?"

"I dunno. What about Conyers?"

"Nothing yet. I'm going to have to talk to her again. Before John Doe 4 turns up in a damned Dumpster."

Derrick pauses. "Was it zoners, Jen?" He asks me like I'd be reluctant to tell him if it were.

"No."

"You sure? Why are zoners looking for you then?"

"I don't know. And I'm sure."

I pause to light a smoke, a blessed distraction from hell. Inhale, drugs, exhale, exhaust.

"You're gonna do a DNA screen on him, right, Derrick?"

Trent groans, thinking about the money, the favors, and the explanations the computer time will cost him.

Yeah, well fuck that. Still, he needs something to ease the pain of doing his job without somebody greasing his palm.

"Hey, maybe the FBI is really into some satanic shit and you can be the one to uncover it."

He takes my smoke from my hand and gets himself a hit. A little one, which disappoints me because I want a piece of him that runs counter to his baby doll's wishes.

"The Feds? The Anti-Crime Mafia? If that's the case, Jen, we might as well pack our shit and head for the hills."

Didi gets me coffee when I get back to the office. Mitch has apparently already left. I am tired, so damned tired. But Didi has news.

"We figured out the gibberish, Jenny. It was actually pretty simple."

"How so?"

"It was jumbled English words, and based upon the passage they were derived from they were simply backward."

"Hmm. Any significance to it?"

"Mitch didn't like it. But let me show you and you decide."

She shows me the gibberish first.

1. *lifeo fcrow na thee giv ewilli andde athunto faithful thoub edays ten tribulation.*
2. *suffers halt thou whicht hings thoseo fnonefear.*
3. *lifeof treeth eof eatto giveiw ill overcomethth athimto.*

And then the reworded English translations:

1. life of crown a thee give will I and death unto faithful thou be days ten tribulation.

2. suffer shalt thou which things those of none fear.
3. life of tree the of eat to give I will overcometh that him to.

And finally the reversed phrases:

1. . . . tribulation ten days, be thou faithful unto death and I will give thee a crown of life.
2. Fear none of those things which thou shalt suffer.
3. To him that overcometh will I give to eat of the tree of life.

"What's the source?"

"The Book of Revelation, according to Mitch, King James version of the Bible."

"Revelation? Isn't that the spooky apocalyptic book of the Bible?"

"Yes. But Mitch left you an E-mail about it. It's on your console."

I need a priest now to understand all of this.

I go to my console and pull up Mitch's E-mail:

Jenny:

Pop culture has always attempted to "interpret" the apocalyptic "predictions" in the Book of Revelation but most serious students of the Bible know that the writings of the Scriptures must be interpreted against the historical period in which they were written. John, the author of the Book of Revelation, creates a highly evocative and metaphorical vision of the apocalypse, but he wasn't prescient, nor was he attempting to be. Most of the images in Revelation appear to relate to actual historical happenings which, although they are not represented faithfully in Revelation, date the authorship of the text at around the year 95 after Christ's death.

Revelation is largely thought to be John's response to the unjust and oppressive world embodied by the Roman empire of that era. So utterly harsh were conditions during that time that John's emphasis seems to be that most of humanity was doomed to suffer enormous harm unless they stood fast and endured and, if necessary, died in the face of atrocity.

I leave it to you to interpret this in light of the facts of your case.

I will be in touch soon.

—Mitch

"Didi?"

"Yeahjen."

"Do you have a Bible around the office?"

"You can get it on-line in a million different ways, like annotated, translated back to Hebrew, interlaced with thoughtful interpretations by televangelists wanting you to send money, y'know."

"I just need the actual book."

"Don't have one. If you want I can print out the passages quoted or the entire Book of Revelation."

"Give me the passages quoted, then the entire text."

"Hard copy or a squirt to your terminal?"

"Both."

"Gotcha."

Zombies quoting the apocalypse, white teenagers being sacrificed. A common drug. A common purpose?

What were the Zombies doing? Recruiting? For what?

Why do they want me? Because I was there? Or because of something I know?

But I don't know anything. An FBI agent's wife. What in the world could she have to do with all this?

Didi interrupts my thoughts. "By the way, I downlinked a Hindustan phonetics program for that last part, you know, the 'truth' thing and all."

"And?"

"Nothing. My terminal practically threw up its hands. Whatever those words are, forward, backward, sideways, I can't decode it."

An FBI agent's wife. The passwords to heaven. Dead boys. Another one all set to die.

I've got to go see her. I've got to make her talk to me.

"There's another kid out there getting ready to die!" My voice thunders at Susan Conyers, suspected mother of John Doe 2. "They're going to bury the third one in a couple of days! Isn't there anything you can tell me about your son?"

"I . . . don't have a son. I have no children. Can't you understand? I have never had any children!"

"Then how did a teenager with your genetic markers turn up dead?"

"It's a mistake!"

"There can be no mistake."

"Then it's a trick! It's a trick, isn't it? Well I'm not falling for it. I'm not. No matter how much you badger me!"

"Why the fuck would dead kids winding up in the street be a trick?"

"Because you want me to tell you things! I'll never tell you anything. Understand? Nothing!"

She's hiding something big, something she refuses even to think about, complete denial.

"There are no police here, Susan. I'm not trying to get you in trouble."

"Yes you *are!*"

"No. Whatever it is, please. Another kid is going to die unless I figure this out."

"I don't care about someone else's kids!"

"Then what about your own child? My God, he turned up dead in the city subway, for Christ sakes!"

"I HAVE NO CHILDREN!" she screams, and then it becomes clear, the thought as clear as a bell in her head.

Guilt, her guilt is palpable. Guilt is something you can identify with, right, Jen? I want to bulldoze right over her emotion to get to the meat of a confession, but I cannot simply dance with her over something like this and then leave her at the party alone.

"Tell me about it," I ask, my voice a whisper.

She is sobbing, her chest heaving.

<this fucking life!> she thinks, then looks at me through tear-streaked eyes.

"I committed a crime," she begins, "that's why I didn't want to tell anyone about it."

I nod, my eyes locked with Susan Conyers's. "Tell me."

"Roughly fifteen years ago I had an abortion," she says simply, and I hug her with the monstrousness of it. Abortion has been illegal in the United States for thirty-four years. Something that Didi said, in vitro fertilization, comes back to me, except they'd need fertilized eggs . . .

In vitro gestation maybe. *In vivo* fertilization. Susan Conyers didn't have an abortion fifteen years ago.

Someone took the fetus.

* * *

"Abortion has been illegal for a long time. How did you manage . . ."

"Oh, Jenny, legality only stops poor people. Making it illegal meant that only rich people had access to it. I was rich. Such things could be *arranged*."

"What made you decide to get an abortion?"

"I decided as soon as I found out I was pregnant."

"What about the father?"

<god no!>

She stiffens. "I can't talk about that part of it. I'm sorry."

"Okay, okay, that's okay. So you decided to have an abortion. What did you do, put the word out? Tell your doctor?" *Plenty of time to probe the issue of the father later, Jen . . .*

"There's a network of people who know about . . . how to get such things. At least there was fifteen years ago."

"But how, Susan? Who did you ask first?"

"My mother, of course."

"And she asked who?"

"I don't know. I was distraught at the prospect of doing this. Mother did whatever was necessary and made all the arrangements."

"And you never knew any of the details."

Susan Conyers shakes her head. "No."

"Who paid?" I ask, thinking about Didi's monstrous search.

"I don't recall. Mother may have arranged that as well."

"Your mom was very protective of you."

"Under the circumstances, yes."

"I need to talk to her."

Susan shakes her head. "My mom died six years ago."

"What about your father?"

"Still living. But Daddy doesn't know about any of this."

"Are you sure?"

"Positive. Mommy would never tell him something like this. I would have forbidden it even if she'd wanted to."

"Why?"

"I'm his little girl, Jenny. I always will be. I couldn't tell him about this. It was disgraceful enough for me to have to go through with it, but tell Daddy? No."

"Hmm." A clue without leads. I continue:

"Obviously I suspect that what you had wasn't an abortion. Someone took the fetus and took it to term. That child ended up dead in the Los Angeles subway on Christmas Day."

Susan simply nods.

"What did you feel when I showed you the pictures? When I told you it was your child?"

"I didn't have a child, Jenny. *I had an abortion.*"

"But . . ."

"There is no but. That dead body's association to me makes me incredibly angry. I have no children, I don't care what the DNA evidence says."

"No desire to acknowledge the past?"

"There's no past to acknowledge. I terminated an unwanted pregnancy. It's my body, my womb. It's my choice, and I don't care what the laws say."

It's a hard argument to argue with. Still she seems

incredibly fragile in her Santa Barbara bungalow with her miscreant husband who's never around. Her tears dried, her back stiff, Susan Conyers ushers me out of her house wanting nothing except to be through with the entire sorry affair.

I can't say that I blame her.

I tell Didi to forget everything but the search for money, and to conduct that against Michelle Winter's assets. Winter is the mother's maiden name. I briefly relate what I suspect about illegal abortions and stolen children.

"Are they really stolen if the mothers didn't want them?"

"I don't know. All I can tell you is that Susan Conyers feels violated by the whole process."

"How would you feel, boss?"

The question stops me short, because in truth I really don't know. Abortion rights were decided when I was two or three years old, and the fundamentalists and right-to-lifers won; feminists lost. That was all it ever meant to me until now. Women's reproductive rights? I didn't intend to reproduce. I barely had ever had sex; with delicious irony that the one successful sexual experience that I'd managed was with someone destined for the priesthood. (Did that make me a righteous lay? So good he didn't need sex anymore? I thought not.)

"I can't say." And what about my child being brutally murdered and dumped on a street in LA? Susan Conyers maintained that she didn't have a child. She terminated a pregnancy. Period. Her connection, responsibility, and emotional attachment ceased there.

"You can't say?" Didi is looking at me.

I nod. "If you can't say"—Didi is shaking her head—"I can't even imagine."

Yeah, well . . .

A rabid dream of being attacked by kitchen utensils and chairs and held down until the Cuisinart, made gigantic by nuclear fallout and toxic waste, comes in re-e-a-ally pissed . . .

"Boss?"

"Wha . . . oh! Must've fallen asleep. What's up, Didi?" *Some dream that was . . .*

"Susan Conyers is here to see you."

"Fine, just let me freshen up a little."

"Boss," Didi whispers, "she looks like she was in a fight or something. She's crying."

Attacked? I'm thinking, and I forget the makeup and mirror and go into the front room.

"Susan?" She looks at me and she's got a beaut of a shiner that wasn't there earlier. Her hands are bandaged (defensive wounds? I wonder) and she stands upon shaky legs.

"I . . . want to help you. In the case."

"What happened to you? Who did this?"

She's swaying like standing up is an effort. "My husband. I told him about what happened with the abortion." She chokes out a laugh. "Needless to say he didn't take it well. Not well at all." Tears begin streaming down her face yet I can tell she hates being this emotional. "It's finished, finally. Been finished for a long time."

"Maybe we need to get you to a medical provider, Susan. Then we can talk about the future."

"There's something I haven't told you."

More?

"Why do you want to get involved now, Susan? You said it was finished for you when you terminated the pregnancy?"

"It was. But I was clinging to it as a secret. I clung to it in the hopes that my quote unquote marriage had a future. Well there is no future. None. So I only have the past to make up for."

"What's done is done, Susan. Nothing's going to bring that kid back to life."

"You don't understand." The look on her face is something I'll never forget; haunted and terrified at the same time.

"What don't I understand, Susan?"

"Before the abortion, when I get checked out, God, this is so hard . . ."

"It's okay. You're among friends."

<twins?>

"It was *twins*, Jenny. They told me I had *twins*." *She is looking at me and all I can hear are her thoughts—*

<where's the other one?>

Ohmigod.

BOOK TWO

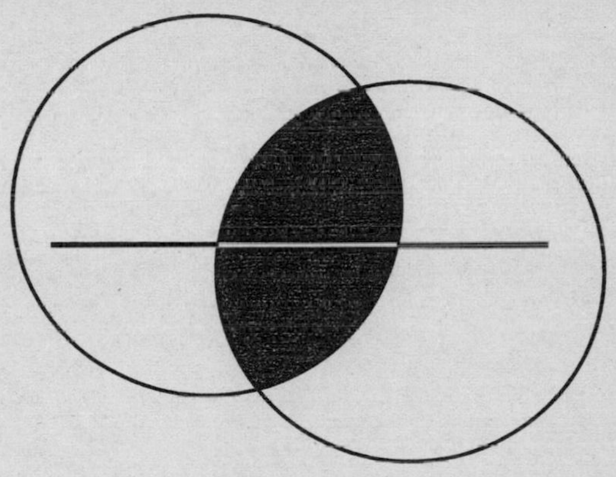

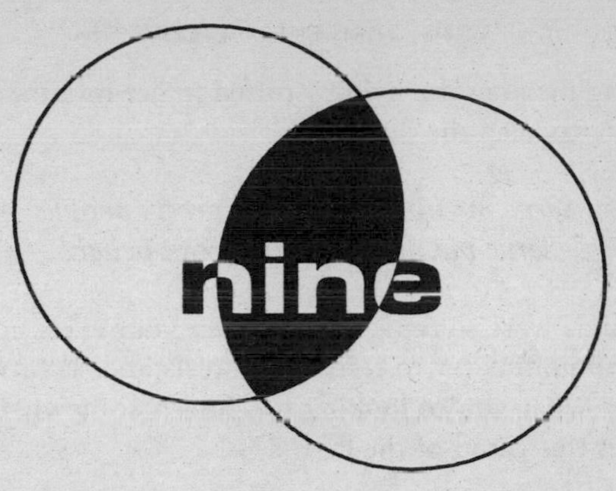

Secret. It was a—

he was vibrating like a guitar string being blasted by a hummingbird's wing while being tuned to a higher pitch. Eyes closed, a bit of sweat trickling down his back, some rolling off his forehead past clamped eyelids—

Where are the bones on that one, yeah

secret. He could smell his perspiration in the clothes that he'd torn off, his shirt was damp in the back. *Hummmmmmmmmmm.*

What if the cure is worse than the disease?

Twitching in time with the music he felt the sad grin spread over his face under his closed eyes. He could smell her a little bit, cheap perfume, perhaps, saliva soaking through the nylons stuffed in her mouth, a foot powder to keep the dogs dry

Serve me up some pretty, pretty people
Serve me up somebody I can believe

his hands were shaking—don't open your eyes, not yet, hmmmmmmm, try to resist when resistance is futile, try to find what you're looking for, find it somewhere else besides this ritual of the flesh . . .

Don't feel sorry for me

a muffled sound like she was calling his name. The bedclothes rustled as she moved around, limited by the restraints on her wrists, the money lying on the sheets between her legs gapped open by restraints tied around her ankles

I hate the look on your face

No one was watching. It was a secret. No one would know.

You say "Just let go"
You say "Come back home"

He opened his eyes. What he wanted was not there.

"Jezebel," he said so softly he barely could hear it over his biorhythmic hmmmmmmm.

"Melissa," she said through the nylon gag in her mouth. He threw another large bill on the bed between her legs. She was smiling around the gag; he was thinking

<I say "I've just fallen from grace">

as he moved forward compelled to find what he wanted; compensation for all pain, release from all guilt, compassion for the failure of youth to endure, sorrow for the losses of loved ones, sympathy for all wishes unfulfilled, all hopes dashed, all diminished potential of life because he could not escape *her* even as he slipped from the cusp of running away to wanting to hurt her, even as his phase changed, as the vibration increased impossibly in pitch, as he surrendered to the inevitability of later being both afraid and ashamed . . .

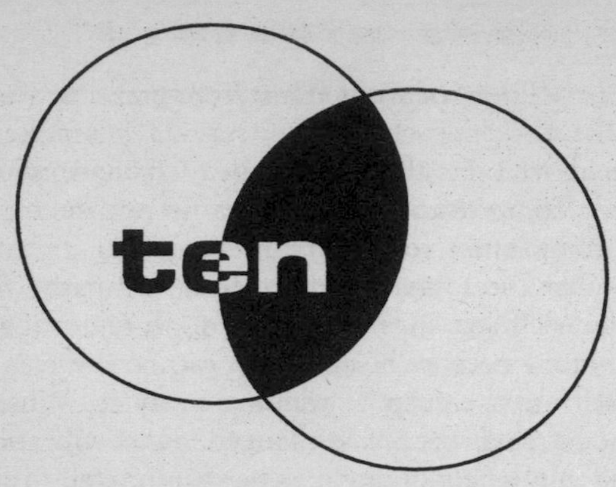

Okay, I admit it. This is so weird that I have to Retreat into Opulence. That's right, go the hell home, have the maid run me a nice hot bath (oh, yes), and be a little spoiled rich girl for a while so I can sort this shit out.

Lucky me. Because I have all this and:

1. Zombies from South Central chasing me.

2. Dead boys turning up without ID all over Los Angeles who probably just happen to be recycled humans from fake abortions.

3. Some serial rapist who has a private channel right into my head.

Lucky me. It swirls all around me, stimulates the senses, makes me feel wanted and alive. Betty, let's talk about buying the Hamptons and making it a seagull preserve. Come by, we'll have tea. Step over the dead bodies littering the yard—next year you'll want to have some, too.

And Betty, you'll never believe how much they cost! That's right. People are cheap. Dead bodies even cheaper. Millions of women just had to give up the right to make a fucking choice. I'm sorry. I misspoke. Men just had to take the choice away from millions of women! We're too stupid to make up our minds about such things ourselves, right? You have the right to remain silent, you have the right to an attorney, you do not have the right to terminate a pregnancy; that's right, you've been screwed!

And what's up with the Zombie thing? What kind of madness has hatched in the zone? And why is it connected to the dead boys? E-e-e-eshh! Another thing to make your skin crawl.

And I'm not supposed to be involved anymore. I'm rich, dammit! My biggest problem is supposed to be which hunk of a gardener to hire to screw on slow days. My biggest worry is supposed to be whether the colors on the helicopter and the Gulfstream match. Look at how I live! Look at who I know!

Chunka-chunka-chunka . . . I can still hear the gunfire breaking up the glassware at the restaurant, the dead man clutching the gun with a banana-shaped clip, cold cold thoughts in his head, *you know the truth* . . .

Man, I don't know shit with a capital S. And what's to prevent them from showing up here?

And Susan Conyers . . . my God I have to feel sorry for her . . . *twins* . . .

Fuck, gimme a narcotic substance and let me sleep through this bad dream—you know like the *Twilight Zone* episode where the plane hits a tail wind and travels through time—just let me come back down through the clouds and see New York the way it's supposed to be, dammit.

Gimme a pill. *A remedy is what I'm seeking* . . .

* * *

Two pills. A taste of what's below. Satin sheets on a canopied bed. Diagramming the cases in my head. Twins.

Susan Conyers.

Zombies.

Dead Boys.

What do they want them for? What is the ritual?

The ritual in the zone was resurrection. *Old mother is alive.* Zombie is a drug of resurrection. Why steal white kids and then kill them with the same drug? Coincidence? It doesn't make any sense. And that doesn't even begin to solve the Who? question.

The Book of Revelation: The prayed-for end of an unjust world. Is that what the zoners want? Why come after me? What do I know, what did I see that's so dangerous?

I saw old mother come alive.

Was she really dead? I saw death in her mind, but does that prove anything? I heard four words that sounded like Hindustan. They called it "the truth." What did it mean?

I saw men juiced on Zombie take multiple gunshot wounds and keep coming as if nothing happened. Does that prove anything? Hell, they could have been on PCP, too, hopped up out of their ever-lovin' minds. Are they really back from the dead? How could they be?

Are you sure you're not jealous, Jen?

Two years ago, during the course of a multiple murder investigation I ingested a viral agent designed to produce changes in cellular structure that would enhance life span almost indefinitely. I am now immune to most things that kill people—cancer, pneumonia, HIV. I can be expected to have a long life before I die of "natural causes."

I am not immune to getting run down by a bus, however. If my eyes can be believed, Zombies are immune to almost anything except severe brain trauma, particularly that produced by a bullet. That just can't be!

I need to talk to someone.

I need to talk to Mitch. He used to be a priest. Maybe he can help me interpret this stuff.

Mitch shows up at the house in jeans and work boots and a long-sleeved plaid shirt. He looks like a migrant lettuce picker from up near San Jose.

"What do you do with your days if you're a defrocked priest?"

He laughs easily. "Look for work."

"As what?"

"A variety of things. An administrator, teacher, counselor, things like that."

"Any luck?"

"No. But I just started looking."

"Well, um, good luck. I invited you over to ask your opinion about some of the things that are going on. I read your note, very helpful, but I need some more depth."

"About the Book of Revelation?"

"Not so much about the Bible itself, but why would these people have that in their heads? What does it mean?"

"It could mean many things. Since the phraseology was garbled and backward, it means that these people are not worshiping the holy word, as such."

"Then what are they worshiping?"

"A concept, a leader, something or someone who

uses these phrases as a talisman to enhance their power."

"A talisman?" *The Truth? The passwords to heaven?*

"A symbol of something they, with their supposedly extrahuman intelligence and calling, can interpret for the masses of their followers."

"It seemed to be part of the ritual." I explain to Mitch what I saw in the South Central Zone.

"And it appeared that they brought the old woman, 'old mother,' back to life?"

"It appeared. And I connected with her for a moment as they streamed past me. It was like connecting with darkness itself, like being able to feel night against your skin. Creepy as hell."

"All of which can be faked."

"Including the telepathy?"

"You don't know what the drug can do. You said in your office it was a fairly potent hallucinogen, that it could be fatal if given in sufficiently high doses. What you saw, what you felt, could have a pharmacological origin and not be the result of some mystical near death experience."

"Then why?"

"I can only speculate. Their appearance could be the result of long-term dosage of the drug. It could be cultivated to induce fear in people, to enhance the sense of their power. Even the name Zombie seems designed to inject fear into the equation."

"Still, Mitch, what do they have to gain? And what about the woman thinking 'the truth' represented the password to heaven?"

"I don't know. Groups form under social stress around a common purpose. Is it a religious purpose? Is it a criminal purpose? We can't know. And heaven? The concept of grace varies with culture and belief. There are lots of conflicting viewpoints on that one. But I've never heard of one that required a cipher to get into."

But the Zombie at the restaurant—"you've heard the truth . . ."

"Why Revelation?"

"Ah. I told you that the significance of Revelation to most Bible scholars relates to the time we think it was written. Many Christians were suffering at the hands of an increasingly tyrannical Roman Empire. It was as if the author of Revelation was hoping for the fall of that unjust society."

"And so zoners could be prophesizing the fall of this society?"

"Praying for it, yes. And who would blame them?"

And so is *The Truth*—somehow the key?

After Mitch leaves I begin thinking about Susan Conyers and the John Doe bodies. I pull from the office server the LAPD files on John Doe 1 and 2 and look at the autopsy notes from the county coroner. There is something that I'm missing, something that ties the bodies to the zone other than the drugs used to kill the dead white boys. Is it the vaguely religious underpinnings of what I saw in John Doe 3's head and the zoners taking passages from the Book of Revelation?

I have a profound and utter hatred for coincidences. I have a profound and utter fear of dead kids, of killings such as these. As I pull the file I recall the abyss in John Doe 3's mind as his brain ceased, his heart stopped, his breathing rasped no more in his chest. What about the wounds in the corpses' extremities? What's the significance?

There is some language in the autopsy files that I can't interpret; I have a hunch that this might be what I'm looking for. I get Derrick on the line. He's at his girlfriend's.

"There were wounds on each of the John Doe bodies that were never explained."

"Which wounds were those?"

"John Doe 1 had a wound in his left foot. JD 2 had a wound in his right palm. JD 3 had a wound in his left palm. All puncture wounds, but you said at the JD 2 scene that they didn't appear to be involved in the cause of death."

"Oh, right. If I had the files I could point out to you what the coroner said, and its significance, which isn't much. You want me to plug into the LAPD net and get the files dumped into my head?" And he's really asking, "Is this all that important right at this second?"

"I'm sorry, Derrick. But I need some answers to the twenty puzzles that I'm trying to put together blindfolded at once. Yes, please access the files, wait"— I stop him before he protests,—"and I will indeed make it up to you."

"Really? How?"

"I dunno, little boy. Maybe I let you ride the pony."

From the look on his face I can tell he's taking that one the wrong way. What's up with you, Jen?

"What was that? I'm pulling the files from LAPD now."

Nevermind . . .

"Okay," he says after a minute or so. "The coroner found no evidence that either of those wounds were puncture wounds. There's no metallic residue in the epidermis like what you'd get from a knife or a bullet. There was also no searing of the flesh that you'd get with an energy weapon strong enough to punch through that much skin and bone and leave that clean a wound."

"So where does this leave me?"

"Beats me. There's a term here I'm not sure I understand. In each case he calls the wounds a purpura, whatever that means."

Purpura? What the heck is a purpura?

Ask me no questions I'll tell you no lies. In my head buried near the neckline my internal processor kicks in, interpreting that thought as a query.

Derrick tells me, annoyed by the way, that the DNA screen on John Doe 3 hasn't turned up any matches to anything. I sign off while the microprocessor in my head dutifully reports—

<Purpura definition found. Replay?>

<yes>

<definition follows: Purpura is a twen-cen term describing largely psychosomatic wounds to the flesh or body parts. Patients with mental illness, acute psychosomatic trauma, etc., have been known to manifest spontaneous wounds or injuries that could not be explained by natural circumstances. Commonly known as psychogenic purpura. —More—>

No more. I need to think about what the hell this means.

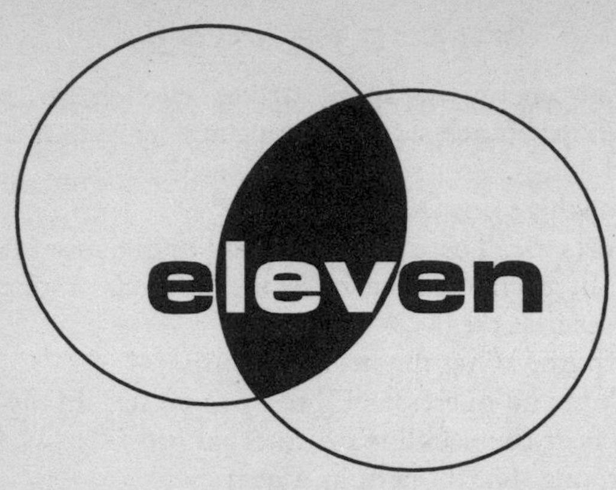

What this all means. The hombre said that I stole the future. Susan Conyers wants to find out what happened to her second child because she has no future. An ancient documentary once talked about idle youth and juvenile delinquents, commenting that young people had "no vision, no faith." A poor boy, a rich woman. A wealthy telepath. Look around; I'd like to know which sick bastard had this as their "vision," and I'd like to know whose prayers were answered by this wreck of a society.

Look around. Fear lurks around every corner chased by a news cam. If real life weren't this screwed up some newscaster would have to invent if for the noon, five, six, or eleven o'clock broadcasts.

Look around. Whose vision are you? What faith got you this far? What is preventing you from having your head blown off in the next thirty seconds? Nothing. Nothing at all. We walk down the street in fear that our tenuous hold on this earth will be erased without our consent. The role of the dice. The role of fate.

My destiny to meet a stranger. There is something at the center of all my disparate threads, my dreams, I can feel it there, unseen but with a distinct pull. What is it?

Who is he?

He was at the center console in his web of sophisticated electronics and computers. He was coding sequences as his mind squirmed.

What did he want? Melissa? *The woman of his dreams?* The blonde? He knew the blonde was real. He could feel her revulsion at the things he did even though he couldn't read her thoughts. He knew she was connected to him. Knew that she was drawn in because of his power. His potency. His secrets.

And because of the drug. Taken in small doses, Zombie had pretty amazing properties. Applied topically, it was an amazing combination of anesthetic and salve that could bring dead frostbitten skin to life. It prolonged erections.

Ingested orally in controlled doses it had connected him to the blonde. He dreamed of her in his sleep, almost every night. He had her inside her head, almost every night. He could send her love letters while he was in the midst of the hunt because he was aroused. She joined with him then. She watched from both sides.

She was the only one who knew his secrets. Why her?

The thought, the word itself recalled his vague dread, his horror that he couldn't quite name and his mind substituted a horror that he could remember. Fighting the gorge rising in his throat he moved to the center of the chamber and strapped himself into the padded couch as the first bead of sweat popped out on his forehead.

He lay down in his chamber of memories, a slender gold thread from the base of his neck leading into the console of his workstation. Unlike the blonde, he'd meticulously catalogued and saved all of his digitized memories from as early as he could remember. His offline memory files were constantly accessible to bolster their neurological counterparts. He called up the directory of the terrabytes of his life stored in the machine:

1. Autobiographical Memories
2. People, Places, and Things
3. First Times
4. Day, Date, Time
5. Secured Topics

And selected

1. Autobiographical Memories

and further chose

Psychological Signatures

and triggered the first item in the database. The machine whispered to him, and he saw, and he smelled, and his mind recalled . . .

It was a short memory. He and his father returning home. The nine-year-old child anxious to see his mother because of an award he'd won in math class. He wanted to be the first through the door, punched the codes on the keypad while his father lagged behind him in the hall. The door opened with a slight whoosh of air that indicated the climate control had the place a little over-pressurized, just like Momma liked it.

The foyer was dark. The entire flat was dark. The door closed behind him and relocked, locking his father out until the older man could work the code. He could hear something thick dripping onto the polished wood floors, then the creak of a hemp rope. His eyes adjusted to the dark—*something was hanging in the middle of the foyer.*

Someone. "Lights on!" he commanded.

He was still screaming when his father managed to cycle the cyberlock and enter the apartment.

He came out of the augmented recollection with a stilled scream waiting in his throat. His father had beaten him for making so much noise, of all things. It was his fault that Momma had done what she'd done.

He glanced at the console. It said:

REPLAY COMPLETE

and he hit the ENTER key. The next option made him smile:

(S)AVE/(C)HANGE/(N)EUROBIOLOGICAL REPROGRAM RECORD?

He hit the N key. Dutifully the computer requested confirmation:

CONFIRM NEUROBIOLOGICAL REPROGRAM? (Y)/(N)

He hit the Y key. Yes.

ARCHIVE COPY WILL REMAIN.

ENSURE SUBJECT IS ON LINE. PRESS "ENTER" TO CONTINUE

He checked to make sure that the slender gold cable

was still firmly seated at the back of his neck. Everything assured him that he was still connected.

He pressed the ENTER key and closed his eyes. Good-bye Momma. He closed his eyes to remember the sight of his mother hanging in the front foyer of their apartment, blood and bodily excretions dripping to the floor, the chair she'd used to position herself in the far corner of the room where it landed when she'd kicked it from beneath her feet. ARCHIVE COPY WILL REMAIN.

But the memory was gone, zapped via the magic of a tiny electromagnetic charge pinpointed into his brain by the computers. His eyes snapped open as he searched his mind to try to recall what he'd just done. Who he was thinking of. All that was left was a vague sense of unease, a murmur, something that he couldn't get his mind's eye around, but the subtle associational clues were disappearing.

The console kept a log of such things, just in case he had to put back in his head something that he'd accidentally erased. He'd thought about reviewing all the memories, of re-creating his life and identity, but he . . .

This one was a bad one, they were all bad, that much he knew. Even though the actual event was no longer part of his organic memory, even though it was no longer part of the microprocessor in his head, the vague disquiet, the dread remained. He was leaving magnificent horror behind, dressed down like the strippers, leaving, changing, disguised and in denial.

His fingers flew to the keyboard. RECALL/NEUROBIOLOGICAL REPROGRAM/LAST THREE INITIATIVES and looked at the list, debating:

1. *Momma/Foyer Scene: Age Nine <Reprogrammed and Deleted>*

2. Melissa/Action Sequence <Reprogrammed and Deleted>
3. Edith Wharles/Action Sequence: Recent Past <Reprogrammed and Deleted>

and ultimately decided not to recall any of them.

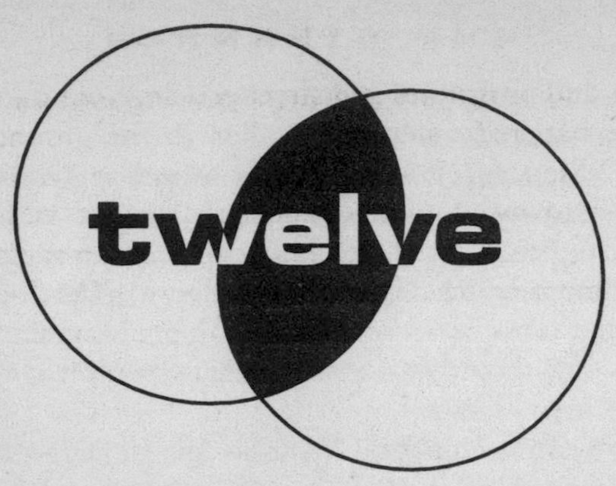

I trudge into the office the next day to rally the troops. So many leads, so little sense of direction. Which way to go first?

Although Mitch and Susan Conyers resist, I decide to go to church. I'm a sweet religious girl, doncha know, and all the religious subtext in this one is just callin' me to get saved, amen!

I argue for the Church of the Resurrection, but Mitch is absolutely against accompanying me there. Should we go Catholic, Protestant, Baptist? Street corner?

Inside and outside the zone there are hundreds of street-corner churches. Reverend Doctor Thisorthat presiding. Gotta hustle for God, amen. Susan Conyers suggests that a "grass roots" church might have its ear to the ground better. Close your eyes, scan the listings under religious, and pick one.

The House O' Prayer is in one of the seedier districts near Hollywood Boulevard. The church of runaways and prostitutes and street people, from the looks of the battered outer facade. Ear to the ground, eh, Susan? Man.

Not to mention the trademark conflict with that House o' Pan . . . well, you know, the breakfast place. It is late morning on a Tuesday as we go in. The door has a ragged cross scratched into it. The rectangular window facing the street is crudely stained with what looks to be Christ's image?

Hey, it's a soup kitchen, too? The homeless bums, the Stim junkies, the hookers, the dopers, are all lined up waiting to get served. There's enough 150-proof stink breath to contraindicate smoking. Screw it, I light up anyway.

"Sorry, miss, but there's no smoking in the church itself." This from a small nut-brown woman wearing an apron.

Many of the clients waiting to get served are smoking. She sees my gaze and answers—

"We are more lenient with our members than with the general public. They will be told about our smoking policy as they are served. Now what can we do for you?"

"Certainly not breakfast. Is the reverend around?"

"He is if you'll tell me who you are and what your business is."

Susan Conyers is creeped out by the symbols of religion. She lights a cigarette and inhales noisily, pointedly ignoring our host's stare.

"We're doing research," Mitch answers. "We are conducting a survey of small area churches."

"I'll get the reverend."

* * *

Reverend William Cappers is a tall reedy thin black man with a dirty cleric's collar. He smiles readily at us and shakes each of our hands. He fumbles with one of my deluxe holographic business cards, glancing at it, moving it to a new angle, and looking at it again.

"What can we do for you?" he asks. There is a note of suspicion in his voice.

"We are working on a case."

"Missing persons?"

I shake my head, no. Susan Conyers says, "Yes. In a manner of speaking."

"Which is it?"

"We just want some background information from local churches that may help us solve a missing persons case," Mitch chimes in.

"Okay. You want to know about my church? Or did you have specific questions?"

"Just . . . your sense about what's going on in the streets. Anything unusual, perhaps?" This from me, as soft a lob as you can get.

Reverend Cappers laughs. "Depends upon what you call unusual. Had a young girl give birth in here last week. Boyfriend didn't even know she was pregnant. Always was a little on the heavy side, wore loose-fitting clothing. We've also had people drop dead from some new infectious disease going around, don't know what the hell that is. And we had a prostitute come in here all bloody—turns out she'd just cut one of her customers."

Mitch: "You make it sound like it's all in a day's work."

"It is."

"Aside from that, anything that you see, or hear, that you find unusual?"

"More of the fanatics in these parts than usual."

"Fanatics?"

"You know, doom and gloom folks, end is near, that kinda stuff. Had a group actually come into the church sprinkling holy water while we were serving people. Called them all 'damned sinners.' "

"Where do these people come from?" This from Mitch.

"You know, the usual. There's some coalition of mainstream churches that's been raising heck for years. People say that's where organized religion puts all their fanatics."

From me: "What churches are members of the coalition?"

"Catholics, Protestants, Baptists, you name it, they're in it."

"And what does the coalition do?"

"Beats me. I've got my hands full just trying to keep my head above water and serve my constituents. I suppose they have meetings and decry the moral decline in society. I suppose they bleet about how much they're doing to protect our moral fiber. That would be typical."

"Know anything about the drug Zombie?"

"Sur-r-e. Low-grade hallucinogen. It's an export from the South Central Zone."

"Is it popular?"

"Not particularly. Seems there's better bangs for people looking to get high."

The good reverend is looking at Mitch, who carefully looks away.

"And do you attach any significance to these passages from the Book of Revelation in the Bible?" I ask.

I show him the passages taken from my memory of

the Zombies in the zone. Reverend Cappers reads them silently, passes them back.

"No more than anyone else. People have been talking about the so-called Final Days for fifty years. For most of my constituents, maybe this is their final days. The average life expectancy of a prostitute or a runaway is not gonna strain the social security system. Other than that, it's the Bible, and I use it the way I use any other part of the good book—to make a point."

"What point?" I ask.

"Depends on the sermon and the circumstance. Say," he finally says to Mitch, "don't I know you from somewhere?"

"No. I doubt it," Mitch replies hastily.

"Wait a minute. Church of the Resurrection! I've heard you speak. That's it, isn't it?"

"I was associated with the Church, yes."

"Yeah, I'll say. I can understand you not wanting to talk about it. C of R is big in these interdenominational councils. I can't say I agree with the message."

"Many do."

"But you didn't." *Cappers seems incredulous for some reason . . .*

"That's one of the reasons I'm no longer affiliated with the Church."

"What precisely is the message?" I ask.

"Decline of society, decline of morals. Racial hatred. And these C of R guys . . . number one self-righteous with a bullet."

"What's wrong with deploring racial hatred?"

"They don't deplore it, miss. They encourage it. And these C of R guys have bodyguards that would make the gun nuts blush with envy."

I look sidelong at Mitch. Could this be true? Holy rollers packin' heat and talkin' racist trash?

Mitch, of course, doesn't look at me. Screw it, I ask the good rev here another question.

"Do you see anything similar in the zone? You know, religious types with a subspecialty in armament?"

"South Centro is an armed camp. Either you have a gun or you're under somebody's thumb. Religion? Gangsta religion maybe. Almighty dollar religion maybe. Whispers of other things, weird things, but that's fear, mostly."

"Fear of what?"

"Fear that when He comes back, He's going to be very, very angry."

Wandering around the church led Susan to reminisce a bit, maybe it was her sins in a place of redemption opening up around her, who could say?

Of course her father loved her. Loved her enough to lie to her and tell her how pretty she was, even when the evidence in the mirror told her otherwise. She wasn't ugly. She wasn't particularly acne scarred, not particularly tall or short, not particularly fat or thin, and not particularly attractive, either. She knew this. Her parents knew this. They all hoped for a fairy tale, that's all, someone who would marry their Susan for her personality, yeah, the person that she was inside. Someone to satisfy the romance imperative.

When she became engaged to Robert, who was about to leave for FBI basic training at Quantico in Maryland, they allowed themselves to believe that their fairy tale had come true. At least her parents believed it. Robert wasn't rich, but he was good-looking with an honorable profession ahead of him. It worked to tell friends and associates and people she met that her husband was an FBI agent—it had a certain cachet. The twenty-first century was the province of law and order, after all.

"Her?" Robert had asked when they were about to be introduced by a mutual friend. He didn't know that she could hear them speaking although he hadn't tried to hide his disappointment. And it was impossible to miss the mutual girlfriend rubbing her thumb against her index fingers to indicate "money," impossible not to pick up the instant change in his demeanor.

The subtle insults and gamesmanship continued right through their whirlwind courtship and the early part of their marriage. Susan learned quickly not to attend FBI functions because Robert spent most of them twisting his wedding band and flirting with somebody more attractive. She overheard too many comments about her FBI-gigolo husband that she was meant to "accidentally" overhear.

But in the end, yeah, so what? If you added a dead departed loyal dog and a stolen Bible to a lousy marriage you could make yourself a country western song. Miss Plain Jane had snared a husband, and that was important to Daddy and therefore important to her. People had suffered worse, and by the end Robert was just a detail. Really.

But a kid?

The more she thought about it, the more she concluded that a child was something else entirely.

We left the good reverend's church. Mitch was distant, Susan Conyers self-consumed. I vetoed the idea of making more rounds to local churches. I wanted Didi to do some net bending about the Church of the Resurrection and its former leader, Mitch Belford.

We trudged into the office less than a happy crew, and I for one was not sure what, if anything, we'd accomplished. Didi made coffee (I lied to myself and said that this was simply because of her facility with the equipment) and we sat around and stared. Didi pulled me aside.

"We got a hit on the money trail for the abortion, boss."

"Yeah?"

"Uh-huh. Doctor's name is Staley. Malcolm Staley. OB/GYN. Works in the valley."

"Which medical provider is he associated with?"

"A bunch." It figured, actually. Cost containment being what it was, physicians needed to ally themselves with a number of providers so that the fees from theoretically servicing large numbers of healthy patients outweighed the time and cost of actually providing care to those that needed it. Unless you were really rich, going to a medical provider was like going to the bank. You waited, and hoped that the people in front of you in line weren't doing too many really complicated transactions.

Another clue, another link in the chain. How best to approach it? Walk in and ask the good doctor if he arranged abortions, and could he please arrange one? Take Susan in and see if she recognized him?

"Can you get a picture of the man?"

"Sure. Shall I show it to Susan?"

"Nah. Not yet. I need to think about this."

"Okay. Anything else?"

Sure. Spying on your friends, Jen. "Yeah. Dig up why Mitch Belford left the Church of the Resurrection."

"When did he leave?"

A shrug from the all-knowing all-powerful former boss. "Recently, I think."

And, surprise, surprise, something akin to irony from Didi?

"Thanks for narrowing it down, Jen."

"Anytime, pardner."

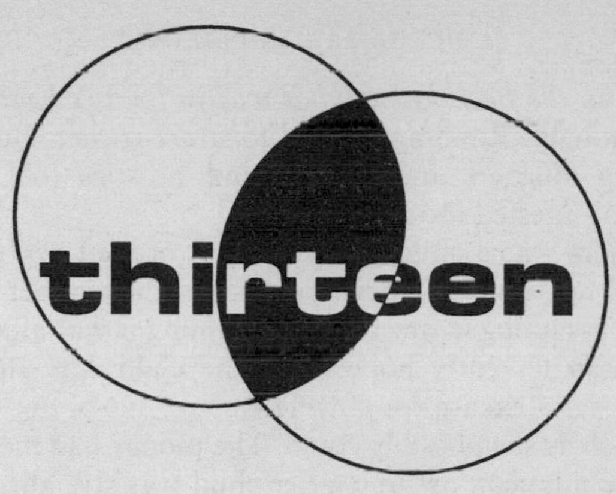

And so here we are, just one happy crime-solving family. Susan Conyers looks like a scared rabbit. Mitch is handsome, but something about him doesn't get the juices flowing. Me, I'm a wreck from not enough sleep and too many weird things. And Didi shall inherit the earth, amen, looking up dirt on Mitch.

"I wish we had more direction," Susan Conyers says, lighting a cigarette.

"That's the kind of thing men say about women, Susan. We have direction. We just don't know which one it is, yet."

"What was the point of going to that god-awful church with those people? What are we looking for?"

"A link, a clue, something in the air that makes all of this make some sense. Hell, I'd go to Rome if I thought the pope could dispense some wisdom."

"I'm lost, Jenny. I'm sorry to say it, but I'm lost."

* * *

Who the heck knew what was in Jenny's head? Susan thought. Running around to street-corner churches serving muggers and junkies and prosties (oh, my!) maggot-infested food? For what?

There was a child out there that needed her. Okay, maybe not a child. Fifteen years old. Ancient. Set in his ways, assuming it was a him. Assuming it was alive.

Susan fervently hoped that the child was alive. It was a valid excuse for cutting Robert out of her estate as much as she possibly could. The money had meaning for the moment, assuming her child was still alive. She could give it everything.

She could give her father a grandchild.

"Jesus Christ! You got pregnant behind my back? You broke the law? What the hell—" and then the torrent of verbal abuse came. She took it silently, the pain a badge of honor in a way. This was just the final insult in an indefinite string of insults because she wasn't particularly attractive. Except for her mutual funds and investment portfolios. Those were fucking gorgeous.

Would the baby care?

<It's fifteen, stupe.>

About the abortion?

Mitch: "We're all lost, Susan. Something will happen and we'll get our bearings."

"Some poor kid will die, you mean."

This from me: "Maybe. Maybe some poor kid is already dead."

"I just don't know where to start to put the pieces together."

I can help with that. I go to my office and dig out the diagrams of the disparate cases. I leave the rape case neatly hidden in a messy drawer, amazing how that can happen.

"Here," I say to Susan, "this is the way I do it. Remember set theory from school? Well, this is set theory. Everything in the circle is connected, everything out of the circle isn't connected. Where things intersect, we find causes, people, or things that have influenced the other circles."

Susan, looking at the diagrams. "Bob used to talk about hating getting involved with women. He hated being tied down to a woman. He always talked about women being victims, like sheep, and that getting involved with a woman was like marrying a victim. Oh, the crime maybe hadn't been committed yet, or maybe it had, but one way or another, either the man is blamed for it, or he has to suffer through it like it was his own pain."

Me, half under my breath: "Guy sounds like a fucking prince."

Mitch: "And what did he say about men?"

"He said if women were victims, men were wolves. Meat eaters, fighters, kill-or-be-killers. Wolves don't marry sheep, they eat sheep. He always used to say that to me. Sleeping around, not coming home. I can't live with sheep, he always used to say."

"So, lemme get this straight. Does he think that women should be more like men?"

"According to him, it would make us more compatible with them, yes."

"Remind me to fuck everything that has a pulse."

Mitch: "Not your nature, is it, Jenny?"

"Nope. I like to think I'm more selective."

Susan: "Well, Jenny, I guess there's just one word for you."

"Oh, yeah? What is it?"

She smiles. "Baa-aaaa."

Didi busts out laughing. "Very funny."

"No," Susan Conyers says, "not funny at all. I gave up my freedom and my life for a man that called me a goddamned sheep and who didn't respect me from day one. I kept his house, I cooked when he honored me with his presence, screwed him when he wasn't fucking someone else. This isn't the life that I signed up for. It wasn't even life at all, really."

Mitch: "What did you want? I mean really, down deep?"

"I wanted the life my parents had, the life my mother had. I wanted a man who wasn't perfect but who loved me and needed me. I wanted a relationship that could endure. I wanted happiness."

"Through a man and marriage?"

"Yes, of course. I never considered a career because money has never had to be a goal."

From me, a whisper: "And children?"

Susan exhales smoke in a long sigh before answering. "Yeah. Sure. Kids. I know what I did was wrong, but I had no other choice in the matter. I didn't. Now I just want to put it right, even though nobody is going to put my life right. No one."

I think of her in her neat little Santa Barbara house, a dream home for 85 percent of Americans and a 110 percent of the people living in the South Central Zone. The order, the neatness, the sunshine pale in the afternoon of my first visit. Her life story is that she kept the house neat and had a gun for the bimbos that came by looking for closure over her shithead husband.

"We think we found the abortion doctor," I say, and it comes out so nonchalantly that I am surprised that I said it.

"Really?"

"Yeah. Dr. Malcolm Staley in Beverly Hills. Name ring a bell?"

She shakes her head. "Nope."

"Would you recognize him?" I nod to Didi to get the picture she pulled from the net.

"I don't know. I was pretty sedated through the whole thing, even before the, uh . . . procedure."

"Didi found a money trail from your mother to this doctor about fifteen years ago. It wasn't that much money, but it was significant enough that it stood out. No transactions before or after that we can find. Just the one transfer."

"Then maybe it's him."

Didi hands her the picture of our would-be abortion doc to the rich and famous. He's older, in his early sixties, his hair still black and full; a pencil-thin mustache on his lip. Susan smokes for a while in silence, studying the photo. Then she shrugs.

"I don't know. Maybe we should go see him. See what he says."

"Um, he won't say anything. If he's dirty he's probably perfected an air of plausible deniability for at least a decade. What I'm going to have Didi look for is transactions similar to yours in his records. Then we can go see him."

I go home. Lush grass, expansive lawn, burly security people whispering into their heads as my limo-on-call cruises through the gate. Mama-san is home. Alert the media. The house looks impressive lit up as it is at night, floods focused on the front entrance with the damn waterfall going and laser light that plays off the water. The water shuts down as my limo approaches because I don't feel like getting wet just to walk in. Maybe I should change the facade back to the way it was before the stupid party. My security geeks suggest that a more traditional front would enhance perimeter security for the house itself.

I tell cook that I will take something light and tasty in my chambers. I tell com to hold all calls. I'm unplugged from the ubiquitous com net myself, the tiny sockets at my hairline are empty and remain so most of the time. The party seems like eons ago. I ignore my messages.

I go to bed early.

Old people gamble. Life and death on the fall of cards. Jenny, white haired fat and whiny, clutches her cards and creases them, the dealer rebukes her more than once. Not baccarat, blackjack tonight, the fateful twenty-one.

"Fucking century since I was that old!" Old Jenny exclaims. She looks at her cards. A king down, a nine showing.

"Hit me."

The dealer spins an ace from the deck. Twenty.

"Hit me again."

Another ace. Twenty-one.

Jenny wins. She thinks. Dealer calls for bets before he turns his own cards. Jenny pushes all her chips into the center of the green felt table. Old people look and point at her. The dealer—what is it about him? she wonders—looks to a pit boss who nods. Her bet has been accepted.

The dealer has the ace of spades showing. Looks at his hole card. Flips it.

Face card. Not just twenty-one, but a jack, the jack of spades. Blackjack.

He looks at her. His face—he has no face. Just a blur of features. "You lose!" he says.

Door at the far end of the room bursts open. Cuisinart on wheels, seven feet tall, bursts in without sound, just the squeak of rubberized wheels on the rubber mat leading into the room. It's coming straight for Jenny, leaning forward slightly, just enough to see the serrated blades in its mixing chamber, the glass is frosted with brown blood. It comes for her—

—is in her face. "I'm gonna fillet you, dammit!" it screams and the blades start up like a chain saw or something, high speed. Metal on metal.

"No," Old Jenny says, and she tries to get up and her chair falls over. She picks it up, sets it straight. Neatness counts. Sheep to the slaughter. You're going to die, Old mother.

Cuisinart man bends over, scoops Old Jenny up in his mixing chamber. Young Jenny screams, but the dealer with no face has his hands over her mouth, a third hand moves down her buttocks, a fourth hand caresses her breasts. "You're going to die, Jenny! You're going to—"

The blades start up again with a roar and Old Jenny is sucked away from the lip of the glass mixing chamber in a fog of blood and bone and gristle . . .

<suffers halt thou whicht hings thoseo fnonefear>

I gag with the end of the nightmare, try to sit up in my bed, but there is a hand over my mouth, black men in my bedroom standing around my bed. They force my mouth open and I scream, but they are pouring yellow liquid in me, and all that comes out is a sputter.

I spit bitter juice and wrestle away from the hands holding me down, they have strength only in numbers, they have only withered limbs to hold me

<old mother wants to see you, white lady>

and the bodies part as I struggle to my feet on a $1,500 mattress. Old mother is standing by the picture window holding an automatic weapon and a death grin—she has no eyes. Am I dreaming still? I wonder as the weapon in old mother's hand kicks and slugs tear holes in my expensive mattress and satin sheets. Off the bed, dream or not, kick the first *brother* in the groin, yell "Security!" at the top of my lungs. Even though I'm not plugged in the aural monitors in the house should pick up my scream. The cavalry should be coming, should be breaking down the door any minute now, how the *fuck* did these bastards get in here?

chunka, chunka, chunka . . . Old mother obliterates two of her own and blasts pockmarks in the sheetrock. I duck, the train of bullets follows me clumsily, I grab another brother and use him as a shield, and old mother takes him out, vibrations as the shells slam his wasted body, his eyes rolling up in his head, his look—

Ecstasy? Night table explodes from the bullets, wood splinters bite my ankle and it hurts . . .

Yeah. Pain.

This isn't a dream.

Run on the old bag, old mother, old Jenny to the blades to get cut up, damn I wish I had a gun, the Uzi swings 'round, I leap at her through the others who surround her and try to grab my nightgown . . .

A touch of cold, cold flesh. A hint of what's there, thoughts in a rush.

A message from the high priestess of my terror.

<you want the Truth> She spins me around and shoves me toward the terrace thinking, *<tell your boyfriend this is your Truth>*

I stumble in flight, old mother's shove sends me ballistic somehow, the strength amazing. Zombie flows through my veins, and I am linked to old mother like I'm linked to the stranger, images, words, sounds that I cannot comprehend flooding me.

The Truth . . .

Four Hindustan sounding words.

. . . Can not be repeated . . .

Next stop, picture window, too much momentum to stop, so I turn, try to take it with my shoulder . . .

It spiderwebs with multiple bullet impacts just before I hit . . . *heavy weapons* I imagine as I cartwheel head over heels . . .

The glass explodes as I tumble through and down onto the brick-lined terrace that looks over the front lawn. I'm careful not to do a full combat roll with all the glass around and take most of the impact on my shoulder.

Need a gun and a way out. No time to be stunned. No time.

The Zombies are moving toward the window, shuffling forward. I stand, careful of glass that surrounds me and my bare feet. The sound of gunfire on the lawn forces me to turn around.

Old mother a shout in my head—

<Judgment is your Truth!>

The sight sickens me. Security won't be here anytime soon.

My front lawn looks like a war zone. Bodies, some black, some white, are everywhere. A downed helicopter burns off to the left.

They must have missiles. How? Holes have been blasted through the perimeter wall half a mile from the main house. More Zombies are making their way across the great lawn toward my home. They all carry guns. They are shooting every white person lying in the grass just to make sure.

The broken glass crackles behind me. One of them has climbed through the shattered window and is coming for me. His feet are hemorrhaging badly by the time he takes two steps.

<lifeof treeth eot eatto giveiw ill overcometh th athimto>

Yeah, well screw you. The terrace is bordered with a waist-high brick wall. I jump up on it, begin scrambling away from dusty black hands. I need to plug in and call Didi but I can't because I need both hands held away from my sides to maintain my balance.

The wall dead-ends at the front wall of the house. There are other bedrooms and windows within reach, but they all have shatter-resistant glass. I could jump at one and bounce off and down twenty-five feet to the shrubs below. Not a pleasant thought.

And they are coming. Oh, yeah. Their feet must look like raw hamburger.

Gotta make a move, Jen, gotta make it . . . oh, God, a second wave of dizziness staggers me, and I can only think . . . *Zombie* . . .

The vision comes over me strong, too strong to resist. I cannot tell if I'm falling or not. The mansion disappears, replaced by . . .

. . . him. I'm in his body, feeling him as he impales a naked woman tied up and spread-eagled under him. She is grunting, blinking the rain of his sweat from her eyes, smiling at him, and I can see the serpent's tattoo on his arm holding his torso above his lover's body, the sensations of a woman discrete and liquid and warm, the warmth is tender and inviting. This isn't rape, but he thinks the name *<Jezebel>*.

I transpose, trying to look up at his face, but he's kissing my neck, my head is turned, and I can feel him inside of me, feel him as he groans, ready to explode . . .

The Zombies reach me on the ledge at my house and my balance fails. They pull me down from my perch bowlegged because I can still feel the stranger having an orgasm, the blacks and the stranger phase in and out of my mind, flashing between murderous dead zoners and my rapist/loverboy, pure rage is all I have left, *uh, uh, her thoughts—*

<fuck me>

and her moans, *uh, uh, uh,* as the stranger takes her, Jezebel indeed, the Zombies coming, the rage. The rage. The rage.

My rage. I scream, bowl the Zombie nearest me over, force my legs to first close, then run, my fist under one's chin snapping his neck back, knee to another's groin, wrench an AK-47 from another's hands, finger on the trigger, killing

<that's right, like that, oh, uh, uh, Uh>

killing, a stream of bullets as I fight the trance and the stream of semen pouring from his loins into his lover's . . . I turn to the window adjacent to the terrace and blow it out, too many of the zoners around me now, to the ledge, jump as my legs spasm from the agony of wracking ecstasy, through the window beyond. Gimpy footsteps approach. Zoners. Zombies.

My head clears. The trance dissipates.

Zoners. In my house. Coming for me. Run.

Run until the authorities get here.

They've killed everyone. Cook is dead, a knife planted in her back, her eyes open in shock, her white apron dark red with arterial blood. Manny, my butler, sprawled on his side, his body cut almost in two by multiple hits. Evan, my chauffeur and handyman, stabbed repeatedly, lies in a pool of blood that looks like wine against the marble floors. I can hear the roar of the waterfall as I run, I can hear zoners behind me, hear their thoughts:

<lifeo fcrow na thee giv ewilli andde athunto faithful thoub edays ten tribulation . . .>

One of them throws a Molotov cocktail down the hall at me. Yellow flame licks the drapes, and in a *whoosh*, flames rush toward the ceiling. Another cocktail pools fire in my path, another smashes against the wall to my right, another catches the hem of my nightgown as I try to leap out of the way. I turn around and loose a burst from the old AK-47 but only a few rounds fling themselves at my attackers before the clip runs dry. Somewhere behind the flames are building to a roar, they've torched the house, dammit, as flames run up the side of my nightdress and singe my elbow. I run, hoping the wind created from my motion will beat the fire out because I have no time to stop and roll on the floor. They would have me then.

Someone behind opens up with a weapon and bullets whiz past me. I stop to tear at the burning skirt of my nightie, run toward the waterfall, more Molotovs burst around me and the heat envelops me like a solid wall of superheated air. The waterfall is my only hope; my nightdress still burns. There may be a gun somewhere near the entrance. Run, Jenny. Run like hell. My legs ache from running.

A Molotov hits me in the back three steps from the waterfall. The *whompf!* from the ignition pushes me the last yard into the water, my back aflame.

And through the other side. Soaking wet, my back aching from where the Molotov hit me. My hair is singed. Somewhere on the second floor fire explodes and the acrid smoke roils down into the foyer. One of my security people lies dead on the marble floor, automatic weapon clutched in his hand. One of the new models that pushes an incredible number of subsonic rounds out of an oversize magazine.

<lifeof treeth eof eatto giveiw ill overcomethth athimto>

They are coming. The waterfall flows swiftly—the conflagration hasn't gotten to the recycling mechanism yet. I snatch up the minigun. As the first zoner's hands appear in the waterfall, I think of my recipe for revenge stew:

Start with the bodies of the undead. I pull the lever on the minigun.

Add water. Several of them are splashing through the water . . .

Season with lead. I pull the minigun's trigger. Shells boil through the sheets of aqua and the runoff basin turns pink with blood. Flames curl up to the ceiling. I can hear the roar of flames from beyond the waterfall.

Bring to a boil. Somewhere below in the bowels of the house the power plant explodes.

Derrick Trent rushes through the door with a phalanx of heavily armed cops. Gently pries my fingers away from the minigun. Hushes me, because I've been making machine-gun noises with my mouth for some minutes since the minigun ran out of bullets. Drags me away from the flames and the destruction and the bodies and lays me down on the cool front lawn in the middle of a beautiful LA morning, dew mixing with blood on my luscious grass.

But I clutch his hand. "Where are they?" I ask, remembering the squads of Zombies roaming the lawn killing the white bodies again and again for emphasis.

"There was no one left alive when we rolled up, Jenny. Lay back. You're safe. Derrick's here."

No one left alive? There were dozens of them in the house, on the grounds. I stand bolt upright to make sure that I'm not crazy—there are bodies all right. Dozens of them, like I'd seen from the bedroom terrace, black and white integrated at last in death and dismemberment.

The effort to remain upright is too much. I sink back down to the grass, spent, unconscious.

"Jenny?" Derrick stands over me waving smelling salts under my nose. Ugh.

"What the hell?" Sit up. Stare at the burned-out hulk of my mansion. White sheets cover the bodies. Forensics teams weaving through the killing field, firemen hosing down what's left of my life as a rich bitch.

"How the hell do a bunch of zoners get heavy weapons, Derrick?"

"It's common knowledge that South Centro is a hotbed of illegal guns, Jen. It's part of the economy. You can buy or trade for just about anything."

"That doesn't explain how these folks got missile launchers."

"Gangs, for example, trade on fear or protection. You scare the bejeezus out of a large enough group of people, and you can demand they give you guns in return for leavin' them alone. And that's not the only way."

Missile launchers. Transported out of the zone to here. Why? How? *The Truth?*

"Jenny, someone here wants to talk to you." Derrick yields and a portly man with a briefcase, an old-style ancient scuffed leather model with a strap and a clasp that closes it, steps into view.

Hands me a holo card.

"I'm your insurance agent. Hollis."

Well that was quick. "You going to issue me a nice big check right here?"

He looks embarrassed. Hesitates. "Uh, no."

"Too many zeros, huh? I gotcha."

"Ms. Sixa, I don't know how to tell you this, but your policy is useless under these circumstances."

"What?"

"Our standard policy for wealthier clients permits them to self-insure against loss that includes the deaths of two or more of their security contingent." He looks at the white sheets festooning the lawn. "Saves a ton on the premiums, you see.

"Unfortunately, I counted fifteen of your security forces dead, including the chopper pilot and the reinforcements sent in by your service. That, of course, frees us from liability for direct property damage and loss of life. Your security service is responsible for the deaths of their agents on your property, although most of those standard policies also have a rider disqualifying coverage involving large-scale loss of life. Worse, since the mayor has declared this a full-scale riot, the 'acts of God and civil disobedience' clause means that you aren't even covered for the collateral damage your neighbors incurred. I'd suggest you get a good lawyer in a hurry because the civil suits alone could run you tens of millions of dollars. In legal fees."

"I . . . I'll sue the security service for letting this get out of hand."

Hollis shakes his head. "Given the high probability of civil suits against your security service, they are probably looking at bankruptcy and an immediate freeze on their assets pending litigation. The grieving survivors alone are sure to petition for millions. I predict there won't be as much as a coffee cup left to collect against there."

I'm still rich. I'll rebuild it myself.

"You are a woman of substantial means, Ms. Sixa. Plaintiffs against you know this. Much of your fortune will survive intact, even after claims, counterclaims, litigation expenditures, and the costs of rebuilding. But as much of a third of it will disappear over the next seven to ten years as the court cases play out, and the rest will most likely be frozen by any one of your claimants litigating against you. Right now, someone's probably in somebody's court asking for a presumptive writ to separate you from control of your assets. This is, after all, the twenty-first century, and our country has more starving lawyers per capita than any nation in the history of history. The laws have changed to ensure an equitable distribution to that underprivileged class once the ambulances start rolling."

"And your advice?"

Hollis smiles. "We can write you a policy right now that will cover all of this and cost you only twenty-five percent of your net worth. This will also allow you to retain control of most of what's left. Still a substantial fortune, by my office's calculation. And less than the eventual cost of what's coming. And so much more convenient. You could continue your lifestyle and rebuild virtually without interruption."

He leans down to stick his face in mine. "Unfortunately, we need your signature on the forms *now*, before the first writs are issued. After all, you can't sign over to us assets that you no longer control by judicial ruling." He thrusts a sheaf of papers in my hand and a pen. I feel like I have no choice. I start signing.

And stop after the third or fourth signature. "How do you know what's likely to happen so quickly?" It seems a logical question.

Hollis smiles. "I know it with certainty because First Federated Insurance is a vertically integrated litigation and insurance firm with nearly one hundred percent market penetration with the wealthy citizens of California. Once the reports started coming in, we dispatched agents like myself to your neighbors and attorneys to courts with instructions to institute the proceedings I mentioned on behalf of our other policy holders. The person filing the presumptive writ against you? His name is Ralph. Nice guy. Sits in the cubicle next to mine. You sign, and I tell Ralph to call it all off. It's that simple, Ms. Sixa."

Fuck! So I sign. I sign until my hand cramps. When I'm done, Hollis, beaming, pumps my hand like he was running for office.

"Oh, and by the way, Ms. Sixa?"

What now? "Yes?"

"Would you entertain selling this property?"

"First Federated into real estate speculation, too?"

Hollis grins. "Nope. I'm interested myself." He takes the papers from me, checks that I've signed everything. "I work on commission. You've just made me a very wealthy man."

Shock is better than even the tastiest pharmacological high. I just lost all of my faithful Tontos, one quarter of everything I own, and endured killing more people than most soldiers kill in a mercenary's lifetime. I probably look like some pale white fish with blond hair, a mermaid in need of suntan lotion.

What do I do? Where do I go? Hollis has assured me that everything's fine, that I'm still rich. I could check into a hotel. A nice sumptuous presidential suite high up in the clouds where no zoners are allowed to work. I could go to the office. I could collapse right here and suck my thumb. That last sounds pretty damn good.

Shock trauma. This is good shit. This kicks some bootay. I don't feel a thing. I can't even think. I hardly know who the heck I am.

Derrick's busy. I could go back to his house, kick the bitch with the perpetual bad hair day out, and jump his normal bones. He'd go for it. Maybe I should go ask him. Oh, looky looky! Didi and Mitch Belford.

"Hi!"

"Are you okay!" Didi asks, then rephrases: "Just how messed up do you feel, Jen?"

My hair feels like a tarpaulin lying on a wet infield as I run my fingers through it. Yuck. "I feel like I'm about to pass out but can't. My bones feel like they're made of jelly. How could this happen to me? I'm rich. This can't be happening."

Mitch puts an arm around me and my legs just go. I can't stand up on my own.

"Let's get you someplace safe, Jenny."

"Safe? Hah! Safe just cost me $100 mil. Let's go someplace unsafe. Let's go to South Centro. Let's kill some more black people who are screwed anyway. C'mon. I had this neat little gun somewhere around here . . ."

"Jen . . ."

"This is my life, dammit! My whole fucked-up life just burned to the fucking ground and I can't figure out for the life of me why! Why? Why me? Why them? What am I, cursed?"

"This isn't your life, Jenny. Your life is today and tomorrow. Not things. Not houses. Not money. Yesterday, ten minutes ago, that's your *past*. No matter what's behind you, it doesn't absolve you of the responsibility for living. We can get you someplace physically safe, but I can't protect you from whatever's in your head.

That's your job for the rest of today. For tomorrow. Forever.

"So what's it going to be? You coming with us? Or are you going to wallow in self-pity?"

Panoramic perspective on wealth creation and distribution. Dozens dead, lawsuits flying. Life no more valuable than spent shells littering my lawn. If this isn't my life then it marks the end of something, and it must mark the beginning of something else. A remedy is what I'm seeking. A stranger is what I'm seeking. Answers to all questions big and small.

He was wired to the gills, cryogenic processors humming with harmonic vibrations. Back in the memory machine, back to psychosurgery. Memories, last three catalogued:

1. Melissa/Action Sequence
2. Momma/Foyer Scene: Age Nine
<Reprogrammed and Deleted>
3. Melissa/Action Sequence
<Reprogrammed and Deleted>

Action Request?

"Replay 1."

ENSURE SUBJECT IS FULLY INTEGRATED INTO REPLAY SYSTEM.

"Done."

INITIATING PLAYBACK.

He lay back on the couch. The images streamed at him as though from a dream. He liked pleasing women; the nature of his crime was that he knew better than they did how much pleasure he could give. Refusing his charms was therefore not an option . . .

She was standing before him smiling.

"Take off your clothes."

"Make me."

Jezebel, he thought, and then he was hot and angry.

He stepped to her, tore open her blouse, revealing the virtua bra underneath clinging to her breasts for dear life. He whispered something and the bra fell away. She had beautiful pendulous breasts with large pink nipples. He was fascinated by their shape.

He threw her onto the bed, roughly tied her ankles to the posts. He tore her panty hose getting it off of her, then stuffed the ragged remnant in her mouth over her protests. Pinched her cheek to get her to give him one arm, then the other for him to tie to the headboard. With effort she spat the gag from her mouth, panting.

<. . . pushed her down into the hard dirt, one hand stroking her between her legs, the other pulling down his pants . . .>

He shook his head. It was a memory fragment, something that he couldn't attach to anything.

He began tugging at his clothes. His pants fell to his ankles and he caressed her breasts . . .

< . . . her name was Edith . . .>

He took a sip of his magic potion.

He groped her on the mattress, feelings stirring, until he was ready.

"Uh, uh, uh, fuck me . . ." she said and he entered her, *oh, yeah,* she said, *oh, yeah, like that . . .*

And he closed his eyes and saw the blonde, the stranger that shared his dreams. Her body was different, more slender, tighter, and she was trying to look at him. He leaned down as he thrust into her and kissed her neck, forcing her face to the side so that she couldn't see him, kept her like that as he fucked her faster, and faster, and harder, and deeper . . .

The images faded and he came out of it in the chair, wired to the machines. At his thought the chair swiveled upright and brought him to the keyboard. He wanted no mistakes as he paged through the memory, looking for her face, not Melissa/Jezebel, the other one.

Image capture and enhance to 15,000 dpi.

IMAGE STORED.

Her head was turned. He typed:

Morph image to full frontal via extrapolation subroutines.

IMAGE AS FOLLOWS.

Her face flooded his head. Blond, very very pretty. He typed:

Archive image.

And the machine responded:

FILENAME?

And he smiled as something struck him, a kernel of knowledge that he couldn't place, couldn't quite *recall . . .*

<filename "Jenny">

IMAGE SAVED AS FILENAME "JENNY."

INITIATE NEUROBIOLOGICAL REPROGRAM? Y/N

He thought about it. Normally he would have deleted the sequence and obliterated the past from his head, since such things troubled him so.

Normally. He quelled the vague disquiet rising in his throat.

"No." He would keep it in his head as well as in the machines, this name, this woman, this Jenny. *A new Jezebel . . .*

MEMORY SAVED.

"Initiate net search match for file 'Jenny' and ID photos/holograms."

PARAMETERS/LIMITS/CONDITIONS?

"None. Find her. Find her wherever she is, whoever she is."

sixteen

They lodged me at the Beverly Hills Hilton. The clerk at the desk managed not to smirk at my appearance when I checked in, just took my entitlements card, ran it through the reader, got a still impressive list of ones and zeros back on the confirm, and checked me into a nice big suite. Derrick Trent couldn't stay long because the police and national guard were talking about mounting a mission in South Centro to take out suspected areas of guerilla activity. (Makes you wonder why they didn't just do that anyway if they knew where guerrilla activity was occurring.) Mitch and Didi I shooed away.

I took a shower and lay down on the bed searching for something not completely mind-numbing on the vid, hoping that I could calm my nerves. Maybe, just maybe, if I let the shock take hold I could get some sleep . . .

* * *

FILE JENNY POSITIVELY IDENTIFIED AND LOCATED.
DISPLAY?

Yes.

The display on his console changed rapidly until her picture came up and a name:

JENNY 6-ALPHA 23799.

and an address. At the Beverly Hills Hilton. Thank goodness for software wizards. He could find anything. *Jenny,* he thought. How had he known?

The answer was simple. He was going to Beverly Hills to find *her*.

Old Jenny peers above the glass mixing chamber of the Cuisinart Man.

—Disappears—

In a fog of bone and blood and gristle as the blades start up

with a chain-saw whine.

Young Jenny held aside by the card dealer with four hands groping her, laughing as she sees herself consumed by the blender, old people come to Vegas to gamble as they die, no hope of winning, just the specter of losing spectacularly . . .

"Jenny."

The dealer whispers in her ear.

"So that's your name. I've finally found you. I'm here, in the hotel.

I'm coming up to see you, lover . . ."

I wake up, hearing something rattling in the corridor outside the suite. My old gun, recovered by Derrick from the ruins of my house, is in my hand blasting away indiscriminately at the door, big chunks of wood veneer and plastic showering the corridor outside. The feeling, the creepy feeling that woke me up goes away.

It was a maid in the hallway. She's not hurt, but after checking with the front desk and finding evidence of my deep pockets, I get a call from a lawyer some hours later.

I refer him to Hollis so he can get in line.

The next day I bully the gang into coming to see me. It's time to get to work.

"It's time to go see the abortion doc. I'm tired of sitting around getting spooked." I say this to Didi, Susan Conyers, and Mitch Belford. They all agree.

"Let's just go in, look around, see if Susan recognizes the bastard, and leave, okay?" The others nod again.

"What ever happened with the search of the good doctor's files, Deeds?" I ask.

"Found a few things. Some transactions that looked like they were possibles, but about six years ago his accountant introduced new security measures. It's almost impossible to backtrack the source of any of his money."

"Shit. Okay. Should we all go?"

"No," says Deeds. "You and Susan should go. Maybe just Susan with a wire. Too many people will look suspicious."

I have to get the hell out of this room and do something. "Me and Susan. Sounds like a plan."

Susan Conyers hasn't said anything and is sitting in the corner quietly smoking.

I look at her, a question in my raised eyebrows. She nods.

Somehow I'm not convinced. Mitch leaves to run errands and I prepare to face the real world.

He watched as they left the hotel, and he naturally concentrated on the blonde. He was perhaps half a block away, sockets at his neck plugged in, software agents whizzing through the various networks that interested him. He heard a chime when her room door locked as she left, hopped from that into the hotel closed circuit security system to watch her exit the elevators. He hustled as he saw which side of the hotel she was going to exit from so that he could be in position.

The thrill of the chase had begun. He would get to know her very well in the next day or so. The rest of it—

—he tried not to think about.

Dr. Malcolm Staley works in a nondescript professional building in North Hollywood peopled with all sorts of medical providers. His suite of offices is on the sixth floor of a ten-story building. Susan Conyers and I walk around the block, nervously smoking, before entering the lobby.

"Recognize anything?" I ask her sotto voce.

"Not really." Her voice is strained, nervous.

"Do you think there's anything here that will upset you?"

She looks at me. "Dumb question, Jenny. How should I know?"

"Yeah, right."

* * *

Mitch telling Susan:

"It's not that we shouldn't strive for better. Our standards are just completely unrealistic. Happiness. Wealth. Children we can be proud of. Love without limits. The very essence of fantasy is that which can't stand up to empirical data."

"Are you saying, pardon my French, that shit happens?"

"I'm saying that our ideals aren't formulated with feedback from the real world. We create a universe where we're the center. So we want a husband that loves **us**. *Children that make* **us** *proud. A life of comfort and civility that ensures* **our** *happiness. This is our fantasy, that we can influence God to provide these things to us to the exclusion of everything and everyone else. There's usually precious little room for real people in our visions about ourselves—there's no room for anything that isn't centered on us. Our key expectation of our relationships is never disclosed because we never ask our lovers to surrender themselves to the universe of US. We never tell the world that we expect it to revolve around us, and if we asked the universe to be at its center the answer would be a resounding NO. And when bad things happen, we are shockingly unprepared for the universe reaffirming this answer in our lives.*

Unfortunately the office waiting room is relatively crowded with a receptionist behind a glass partition sitting at a desk. The door to the inner sanctum is closed, and the receptionist's booth is enclosed. There is no opportunity to see the good doctor without actually going into the back into one of the examining rooms.

"Your name, miss?"

"Sixa. Jenny Sixa."

The receptionist frowns. "Do you have an appointment?"

"No. I was hoping to see the doctor and get a checkup."

She frowns again. "Unfortunately, today isn't the greatest for me to squeeze you in. You see that crowd out there, right?"

"Yeah."

"The doctor is running about an hour behind with his appointments. You can have a seat, but it will be late in the afternoon before anything opens up."

Susan Conyers looks like she wants to bolt this instant. Several hours of waiting? Christ, the frontal approach leaves a lot to be desired.

So shit does happen. She could hardly be blamed, Susan thought, even though after fifteen years she still felt guilty. The forced sex, the subsequent tearful confession to her mother in a hushed whisper in the big house, her mother's look right through her to the *ramifications* for the *family*. The end of the fairy tale.

No, Susan thought, she didn't feel guilty. She would always simply *be* guilty.

"You can't keep the baby," Mother'd said flatly.

"I can't terminate the pregnancy, Mother. You know that."

"Listen to me, Susan. Look at me first so you can understand what I am saying and that I mean what I say." Susan looked into her mother's eyes, so strong, determined, and in control. She envied that sense of control—no, actually, resented it.

"You can't keep some bastard child—you can't even

get to the point where you're showing, for God's sake. Think about your marriage! Poor Robert—"

"I've thought about simply claiming Robert's the father," she said in a small voice.

"And pray this mongrel isn't somehow defective? Is that fair to Robert? To your father and I?"

"There are tests, Mother."

"And the instant something's wrong they'll want to try to pinpoint the reason—your genes or Robert's. And they will know, instantly, that he's not the father. Do you want to answer questions about who the father is?"

Susan said nothing.

"Do you?"

"If you like, we can march right in to your father when he gets home and tell him about this sorry mess you've made of your life, that you are going to have a child that isn't your husband's who may be diseased and defective and that you will no doubt have to raise alone because any self-respecting man would leave the instant he found out the truth."

Her mother stared at her. "Is that what you want?"

Silence.

"And the scandal; our friends, our neighbors, what will they think? That plain old Susan can't keep her underpants on? Merrily having kids with whomever?"

"You know it's not like that, Mother."

"Of course I know. But there's no proof, is there, child? No proof at all. And here you are, after your feeble attempt to sweep it under the rug, this whole sorry affair dumped into my lap—"

"Mother!"

"Don't get indignant with me, Susan. Don't you dare."

"Mother, I think you've said quite—"

"GODDAMMIT! Did you enjoy it? Did you enjoy getting fucked by a stranger? Was it WORTH it?"

She didn't like tears. "Oh, for Christ sakes," her mother muttered, and handed her a scented hankie. The lilacs smelled pleasant against Susan's damp face.

"You are not going to have this child, Susan," Mother said when Susan's face was dry.

"Never mind, miss. I'll call for an appointment."

Susan and I turn to go.

And then I see a familiar face that stops me in my tracks.

She recognizes me, and turns away, not wanting to make eye contact.

A coincidence? Maybe. But this is something that Didi can look into, and just the possibility that it's not a coincidence sends chills up my spine.

Sitting in the waiting room is Edith Wharles. She was raped not more than a week ago.

I wonder why she is here.

Okay, so how about the covert approach?

We go back in the evening so that Didi can plant a smart bomb on Dr. Staley's terminal. A little B & E is good training for a fledgling private investigator, so we scope the building, noting the underground parking garage. We'll try for access through the garage late—

And find it surprisingly easy to get into. Just a card key gate that Deeds diddles with absolutely no problem, managing to turn off the gate's motor so we can (ugh!) lift the thing enough to slide underneath. Didi then taps into the coax from the security cameras.

"Place is remotely monitored. There's one rent-a-cop on-site. He's probably asleep watching reruns of old vid shows."

Damn, we should have brought the sleeping pill-dosed donuts just to make sure. Didi assures me there is nothing stirring.

I pick the lock to the stairwell with a sonic pick that vibrates the thing into an orgasmic opening click. We make our way up the stairs, all the while Didi monitoring the remote station for anything akin to alarm concerning our presence.

Nothing. They ought to sue these people for malfeasance or something. Incompetence? Whatever. This is absurdly easy.

We reach the good Dr. Staley's floor. Sonic pick on the mechanical lock while Didi diddles the electronic mechanism. Both pop open and we swing through into his waiting area.

Didi scans the receptionist area for additional security devices. Nothing.

Ninety percent there. Sonic pick the lock to the inner sanctum.

Shit. Didi rarely curses, but the terminal has a lock on the on/off switch. Rather more effective than a hardware password, at least to amateurs. Let's see if we can get inside the thing and bypass the on/off and power up the hard drive.

Deeds wires around the switch, completing the power circuit from inside the machine. We got power, we got CPU and disk drive booting up. Cool. The monitor asks for a password, but Didi is not going to waste time monkeying with it. She slaps a passive read/write on the side of the slim computer case to read the contents of the hard drive without directly accessing it. The device uses a microvoltage electrical field to read the magnetic patterns of the disk.

I look at my watch. We've already been inside the building for twenty minutes, and my luck would suggest that any minute the rent-a-cop is going to make some rounds of the building. Damn, I knew we should have gone with the doped donuts.

"How much longer?" I whisper to Deeds.

"Thirty seconds to read the drive. Much longer if you want me to put in a software agent. I'd have to analyze the drive pattern and put something in an empty spot to avoid corrupting data."

I shake my head. No good. We need to get the hell out of here with what we've got and get away clean. We can get rougher once we know more. *And I have the damnedest sensation that someone else is watching . . .*

"Finish it up. We're outta here."

It was easy because there was nothing much in the machine. "This is just bullshit office administration stuff, and it's all fairly recent," Didi tells me as we scan the contents of the drive.

I suppress a yawn, then remember Edith Wharles being at the doctor's office.

"Look for a file concerning Edith Wharles, dated today or the last month or so."

"Sure." She hits the keys.

RECORD NOT FOUND.

"Try alternative spellings."

"My search programs do that automatically."

"Okay, try the billing file."

Didi taps into the automated record of where Dr. Staley spent his time this past day.

"Try Edith Wharles there."

"Gotcha." She types, then—

RECORD NOT FOUND.

"Shit. Okay. Are there any gaps in his time for this day?"

"Lemme check."

She pulls up the time accounting program with the day's record.

We both lean in to study it.

"Okay, got there late, like 10:30 AM. Took a half hour for lunch at 12:30 PM. There's some minor gaps of a few minutes here, and here."

"Cross tab those with his phone logs."

"For the whole day?"

"No. Let's reason it out.

"Susan and I got there at around 11 AM. The place was packed then. His receptionist said he was a couple of hours behind on his regular appointments."

"He probably overbooks, then. According to this he was only an hour and a half late getting in."

"Um-hmm. So if I'm Edith Wharles, I come in for an appointment on time, maybe a little early. We don't know how long she'd been waiting, but a couple of hours late would mean if she had an appointment for 11:00 she would have been seen about 1 PM."

"Half hour for lunch, Jen."

"Okay, even giving an extra half hour for lunch, that would put the blank zone around 1:30 PM."

"Try 2 PM."

"Huh?"

"Right here at 2 PM. It's blank. No cross tabs with phone calls. Nothing."

"How long a hole?"

"Forty-five minutes."

Hmm. What would he want to discuss with Edith

Wharles off the record for forty-five minutes? Assuming it was her.

"Can you do a file reconstruct on anything that was erased?"

"Not from this kind of intrusion. A microvolt flux picks up definite hits, not erased files. Child's play to do it sitting at his terminal, though."

"Should we go back tomorrow night?"

"No. By then, the next day's activity may have rewritten the parts of the drive that had the erased data. We'd only get fragments, at best."

"Then I'll have to talk to him myself. Find out as much as you can about his personal schedule. I don't want to confront the good doctor in his office."

The good doctor takes his supper two nights a week at the Beverly Hills Annex Club, a quaint old out of the way haunt of the professionals in the neighborhood who need a place to relax, drink, eat, and play the occasional game of poker or billiards. It isn't some cloistered country club, no membership regs that Didi can find. So the best thing to do is dress provocatively and seduce the good doctor into some conversation, and read his thoughts to the max.

Since I buy Sytogene by the mind-numbing barrel these days, it's somewhat of a shock to be able to listen in on the rabble again. A sheer white minidress translucent enough to put the term "panty line" to shame and high heels, hair in a frenchy deal piled on top of my head. Not quite the whore, but close enough to suggest availability. The good doctor is married; I always find seducing someone who's involved an interesting litmus test of the morals of the species.

The bar to this jointsky is located near the door,

convenient because in the dim lighting I would need some enhanced optics to pick out anything smaller than a Mack truck entering the place. And I have Didi's file photo of Staley committed to memory.

I get the usual not-so-subtle hits. Some plastic surgeon thinks about doing my tits, and I don't mean professionally. Another business type wants to know if I'm looking for some company in a professional sort of way. Clearly not, especially since the barkeep is listening closely to this particular exchange—pros aren't wanted at the Annex. Malcolm Staley, MD, comes in, a rumpled little man with nothing on his mind but his appetite for food, and gets a table in the corner. He is studying something in a thin envelope as the waiter brings him a drink and takes his dinner order.

I ask the barkeep what the good doc is drinking. Bourbon, straight, apparently.

I ask him to put a double together for me, and carry it over to his table myself.

"Mind if I join you?" I ask him throatily. He looks at me—

<hooker? no—looks familiar>

but before he can complete the thought I'm already seated opposite him.

<whoever she is, what a babe . . .>

"My name's Jenny. Yours?" I hold out my hand. He regards it curiously, then takes it, hands cold, I wonder how a man with cold hands does in OB/GYN.

"Malcolm Staley. I'm a doctor." *<and I'd like to do a procedure on you>*

"Please to meet you, Doctor."

He looks at his watch. Waiting for someone? No, just food. *<enough time to eat and slip away with this one? what's the wife disturbance index these days?>*

"Look," he says, his mind already having formed what he's going to say, "I don't know what this is about, but I'm happily married and intend to stay that way." *<innocent denial first, ravishing seduction, next, refusal of whatever she wants after>*

"I'm not here to compromise your morals, Doctor."

<shit. one of those>

"Hmm. Yes, then what are you doing here, if you don't mind me being direct?" *<where's the food?>*

"I wanted to talk to you about certain aspects of your practice."

"OB/GYN people aren't that hard to find. Even given the insurance premiums."

"I have a friend who's in some difficulty . . ." I begin, but this feels all wrong, too direct by several minutes of warming up conversation.

"I see." His mind shouts the warning before he can fumble with the envelope—

<ah, now I know who she is . . .>

And he pulls something out of his envelope.

"Would this happen to have anything to do with this?" he asks, and shows me a photograph.

Security cam shots rarely do justice to my beauty. It's an eight-by-ten glossy of me and Didi, taken last night while we were diddling his receptionist's computer.

"Yes it would." I can hear him, plugged into the microprocessor at the back of his neck, using the net to call the police. *<maybe I can still play this one for some fun . . .>*

"I was wondering when or where you'd show yourself. Saves me a bit of trouble, though. The police . . ."

". . . would be interested in your sideline as an abortionist."

<ooh. a challenge. do-gooders always are . . .>

"They are already interested in how a woman's supposedly aborted child turns up dead fifteen years later." I sip some of the good doctor's bourbon and eye him coolly.

<yeah, right.>

And he eyes me coolly right back. "Look, the only difference between dealing with you and the police is the payee on the check. I've been hustled before and my response is always the same. No crime, no time. The police will only care that one of their clients is being hassled."

He leans in toward me across the table like he's a real operator. *<fuck me or jail, baby.>*

"So why don't you tell me what exactly you're looking for?" In his head he's canceling the police call.

"Some answers is all, really."

"Without an attorney present, Ms. . . ."

"Sixa. Jenny Sixa."

"Well, let me tell you that any "evidence" garnered by an illegal search and seizure isn't evidence in a court of law. And there's nothing that you could have accessed last night that proves your allegation." *<she's got nice legs. wrap 'em around my neck, honey . . .>*

"Are you still in the habit of performing illegal abortions?"

<what i'd do to you is certainly illegal. imagine if she was fifteen. oh, malc, you are such a bastard>

"I never performed illegal abortions."

"Fifteen years ago. Susan Conyers. Name ring a bell?"

"No." *<nor do I recall my patient's names when I spend their money>*

I take a stab in the dark. "What about Edith Wharles? Just yesterday?"

"Edith who?" *<what's with this broad and specifics? I run a health care factory, sweetheart. not some touchy-feely clinic>*

"Wharles. Know her?"

He shakes her head. "Patient records are confidential. I couldn't discuss anyone with you even if I wanted to." *<as if I remember . . .>*

"Why not just tell me why? What's in it for you?"

The waiter places a steaming proto steak in front of him, and I can tell that he's famished.

He can't resist diving into the food on his plate.

"I'm a doctor. Legality or illegality doesn't change the therapeutic effects of certain procedures. Hypothetically, of course." *<like some beef, baby? I bet you would>*

"What does it change?"

"The cost. The availability. The profit. If society wants to regulate it, it doesn't stop the demand. Prohibition in the early twentieth century didn't stop people from drinking, or being alcoholics. It simply changed the dynamics for that group of consumers."

"And that places you in the catbird seat, does it not? As a provider of a service that has been outlawed."

"Hardly the catbird seat. Not given the risks involved. The price and availability simply compensates a practitioner for his or her risk."

"Killing babies is killing babies, Doctor."

He points his fork at me. "There is a moral component as well. A woman in desperate circumstances, her life at risk, would you care to put a price on that?" *<nice, malc. it's all hypothetical, no specifics . . .>*

"Purely therapeutic abortions are still legal."

He snorts. "And disgusting. Once a hospital board

signs off on the necessity of the procedure, the pregnancy is usually well advanced—and then it is killing a nearly fully functioning human being. But there are substantial gray areas that no one will touch, precisely because they are gray. Too much risk. But beneficial to the mother."

"You said when a woman's life is at risk. Those are still legal abortions."

"If a woman gets pregnant by someone other than her abusive psychotic husband her life is at risk. Dalliance equals death or serious injury in such circumstances. And abortions in those instances are hardly legal." *<oh, yeah, ethics. pontificate! I love this shit>*

"And people like you only perform abortions in life-threatening instances? I find that hard to believe."

"It's an inductive proof, however, once you start. If it's true for X, and true for $X + 1$, then where do you draw the line? $X +$ what? What set of circumstances give you, I, or society the right to play God?"

"What gives you the right to break the rules?"

He doesn't answer immediately, chewing a bit, then thinks—

<because the rules are wrong. And people are rarely perfect . . .>

"Then what happens to such fetuses once the procedure has occurred?"

He shrugs. "What difference does it make? It's not a child, not to the biological mother. It's not a living thing, not survivably alive, anyway, depending upon the circumstances. The world is already in deep trouble because of all the errant children that shouldn't have been born given their circumstances."

"Really? Like who? Zoners, perhaps?"

"Possibly. Ours is a society with scarce resources.

Our planet's capability to nurture billions more people is finite. Who says parenthood is an inalienable biological right?"

"The government, for one."

"Yeah? So we can lock them up, put them to death, confine them like cattle? So they can rob, murder, maim? Birth rates at the low end of the socioeconomic scale are burying this country and our way of life. Burying it in a sea of children starved for affection, food, education, opportunity. But abortion is illegal. So is being born on the wrong side of the tracks, damn near. If I'm poor an unwanted child can very well be a death sentence to my ability to make a life."

"And if I'm rich?"

He shakes his head. "If I'm rich, other circumstances prevail, circumstances that are no less pressing than if I'm on the dole, I'm afraid." And he thinks—

<like rape, for instance . . .>

"And what of the aborted fetus? What of its rights?"

"Should an unwanted child that becomes a serial killer have the same rights as one that becomes an Einstein?"

"But who can tell which is which?"

"Exactly the point."

"I don't understand. Besides, most people fall somewhere in between."

"Not true. Look at how well social circumstance predicts a child's success."

"Are you talking fact or conjecture?"

"Conjecture, I suppose. But if the next Einstein is born in South Centro, I doubt we'd ever know it. We do know where the muggers and junkies come from."

"South Centro, you are suggesting."

"Poor, disadvantaged, intellectually challenged people. Wherever they hail from."

"Then how do you justify performing abortions on wealthy people?"

"I never said I performed abortions." *<hee, hee. bullshit is my shield, honey>*

Through gritted teeth: "Hypothetically, then."

"I suppose, *hypothetically*, that I'm keeping bloodlines pure. I suppose that weeding out unwanted children preserves the cachet of the elite. The world needs secure intelligent children whose parents want to be parents. It needs such people more than ever before. It will always need such people." *<and plausible deniability is an art form when practiced by malc staley, md>*

"Then how did a wealthy woman's aborted child end up dead in a subway station fifteen years later?"

"I certainly wouldn't know." *<here she goes with this dead kid stuff again>*

"I think you should."

He smiles. "But I don't, and given that I don't believe such a thing to be possible, I believe there is an error in your logic somewhere, or your data."

But I don't buy that. And Doctor Smug here is clearly the answer to the Who? and Abortion? questions. *<e.g. Him, and Yes>*

Despite being busted by Staley's security cams, I am determined to go back and find real evidence of his abortion business. Back at my hotel, Didi and I talk about what to do and how to do it.

"Obviously there's a secret cache of information about his off-line abortion business."

"And it's completely separate from his regular clinical business."

"What about Edith Wharles? The woman that you had me look up in his computer before?"

"What about her?"

"If she's a client of the nonpublic practice, how does she get transferred from the receptionist's station into his private files?"

"I dunno. What do you think?"

"There's probably an update at the end of the day to merge his terminal with hers, just so that they start each day working with the same information. He could simply have marked Edith's records as not to be duplicated on the receptionist's terminal. He may have his data encrypted with special passwords, things like that. He may also physically remove the hard drive and take it home, or put it in a vault."

"What's the best way to get to it?"

"Knowing which of the above is the case. If Edith Wharles was part of his clandestine practice, it probably makes sense to ask her."

Hmm. Didi, of course, is correct as usual.

But I don't have to call Edith Wharles. She calls me. Angry.

"Are you working for my husband?"

"Nope. Never met the man. Why do you ask, Edith?"

"Because I never told him about how we met. And then you show up at my gynecologist's!"

"Funny you should mention Dr. Staley. I was wondering if you could tell me about your visit with him?"

"No, because you're probably working for my husband. I'm not going to make it easier for you."

"Are you aware that some people think that certain members of the medical profession are connected to an illegal practice of offering nontherapeutic abortions to the wealthy?" This is as close as I'll get to libel and introducing Dr. Staley to Hollis, my insurance agent.

But I needn't have been so cautious. Edith Wharles hangs up in my ear, my question unanswered.

I'm trying to get Ms. Wharles back on the phone when Derrick Trent calls. The National Guard and the LAPD have mounted a successful, or so he says, campaign into the South Central Zone to clear out the so-called Zombies and eliminate them from further attacks across the border into decent white Los Angeles.

I grunt, wondering about the atrocities committed, recalling my own recipe for revenge stew.

"And some rather bad news, Jenny."

Wait, let me guess. Hollis slipped on a banana peel and not only lost all my paperwork but is suing me for the other seventy-five percent of my fortune that his company doesn't already control.

"John Doe 4 turned up. Right at the border to South Centro."

Oh, shit. One beat, two, I'm gonna be sick to my stomach, three beats . . .

"Jen?"

"Where's the body now?" *What if this is Susan's missing son?*

"LA County Coroner's morgue. On ice. Waiting for you."

"Christ. Okay. I'll get over there right away."

I'm shown into an underground lab with cabinets, presumably filled with stiffs. It's cold, refrigerated cold that induces more than a shudder, as if all that's happened to me in the last forty-eight hours has been a race to prevent finding John Doe 4 dead; a race that his killers won, and I lost. Excuses don't really matter much when you're talking about life and death, do they?

The attendant rolls the cabinet drawer open. *Excuses certainly do not matter to John Doe, here.*

With the drawer fully open I look at the shaved head and lifeless face—and look again. "Are you sure this is the correct body?" I ask the attendant.

"Yup. John Doe, brought in packed in ice from an LAPD crime scene not an hour ago."

It's a kid, all right, white male, approximately fifteen years old, but, but, but . . . this isn't the same kid I saw in John Doe 3's memories. Not at all.

I turn away for a second, stunned. Is there another body out there? Could another body already have been found and Trent's trying to contact me?

"Miss?" The attendant doesn't understand any of this.

"Yeah?"

"Ah, LAPD said you were a capable. Said you were going to do something with this one?"

It's a John Doe, just not the right John Doe. Can't avoid doing my duty.

For the record, I check John Doe 5's extremities for wounds. Unlike the others, he has a puncture wound in his right foot. Like the others, it doesn't appear that this wound was involved in the cause of death. I reach down and touch JD 5's scalp, my fingertips just barely caressing the stubble of shaved hair and skin. I close my eyes, waiting for a connection with him, and yet as I sense nothing, I press deeper, harder, searching for something coherent.

But there is nothing. Nothing at all. It's as if everything has been erased. Completely, utterly, totally erased.

Just like John Doe 2. An impossible coincidence, and private detectives don't like coincidences because they don't naturally occur in cases like these. They are part of the repertoire of a sinister actor or actors working offstage while you play footsie with their handiwork.

So how is it possible that Joe Doe 4 isn't dead? How is it possible that John Does 2 and 5 have no memories?

* * *

Didi has news when I get back from the morgue.

"I hacked in to Staley's private terminal, but that's as far as I could get. There's whole sections of it that are separately encrypted with multiple layers of security. I figured his setup would be tight given that there's access from the outside. Probably does some things from home."

"Then we have to go back in."

Didi shakes her head.

"Nope. I've done as much as I can without some keys to the city. We can sit here, we can sit there in front of his terminal. Wouldn't make much of a difference. Without passwords it's all shielded. Even the passive read/write won't work without decryption keys because the data itself is encrypted."

"Then we drag Staley out of his house and make him give us the decryption keys."

"Right. And then we fly away to Never-Never Land on our brooms. How are we going to do that?"

"I dunno. He's married, right?"

"According to you, he said he was."

"Get me a home address."

"The wife?"

"Maybe she has the decryption keys. Maybe she'll be supportive of what we're trying to do."

"Maybe she won't want to risk hubby's license to practice."

"All the more reason to let us get our data and leave quietly."

Didi scribbles something so fast that I can't follow her hands. It's Staley's home address.

Staley lives in a nice Tudor in Beverly Hills. I ask to see Mrs. Staley and the maid admits me as far as the large high-ceiling foyer but no farther. She takes my holo card while I stand there, tapping my feet. I hope the missus sees me because I will resort to rough stuff if I have to.

The maid comes back, my card on a silver tray like a wafer.

"Mrs. Staley wishes to know what this is in reference to."

"Her husband's practice. I need information that's a matter of life or death, and I can't get it any other way."

The maid nods and retreats. Some minutes pass, the maid returns.

"Follow me, miss."

I follow her into the living room, stuffy and overdecorated as if the things had outgrown the living space. Mrs. Staley is a short, wizened woman who looks older than she must be. She waves me into a stuffed wing chair in front of her.

She is sipping a cup of coffee. My card lies on the silver tea service tray that I'd seen earlier. She looks at me closely, a shrewd once-over assessment.

"I took the liberty of calling my husband. He says you confronted him at his club asking questions about abortions." *<which is a relief. you're the type that scandal is made of>*

"Your husband is an abortionist, madam." *<but he's not sleeping with you>*

"I know full well what my husband is and what he is not. What I don't know is why you're taking up my time having failed to convince him of the urgency of your needs."

"It's a matter of life and death. Your husband's records would go a long way toward helping me solve a deep mystery—why children supposedly aborted by people like your husband are suddenly turning up dead fifteen years after the fact. There's a young man who may still be alive whose life we can save if we can just figure out who's doing this, and why."

"You want my husband to risk his practice to help you, true?" *<and you want me to risk everything I have, and everything i've put up with as well>*

"If my suppositions are correct, he risked his practice the day he performed the first illegal procedure on a woman in need. I'm not some right-to-lifer bent on exposing your husband, Mrs. Staley. I just want to know what happened to those fetuses."

"Still, the risks . . ."

"Life and death, Mrs. Staley. What have you got that stacks up against that?"

<everything i've ever wanted> "The life or death of someone already condemned by their biological parent is hardly my concern, Ms. Sixa. I don't see any reason why I should help you, none whatsoever."

I let the disappointment play out on my face. "I may be the first, but I won't be the last. I may be clever, but someone else will pick up the trail, particularly given that four young men, all aged around fifteen, have turned up dead in the last few days. Those bodies pose the greatest threat to your security, Mrs. Staley, not me. How many more before the authorities get curious enough to launch a full investigation? How long before one of your husband's patients comes forward, or goes to the press?

"How long before some 'zine gets a hold of the story and you've got surveillance newscams in your face twenty-four hours a day?"

"Idle threats. The press has nothing on us, and can't do a story with nothing." *<i hope.>*

"What planet have you been living on? Once the press gets the story of the killings, and the fact that these kids have no identities, there will be a feeding frenzy that'll take them right up to your door. I'm your best shot at keeping this thing quiet. I'm your only shot." *Liar, liar, pants on fire. Please believe me, please?*

Mrs. Staley looks at me for a long moment, wheels turning in her head. *<what harm can come of it now? and I know so-o much . . .>*

Then she begins to talk.

Of course, it was her idea, conceived by her and her friends many years ago. Abortion was a service, it was necessary, a woman's right to choose. In the beginning she convinced the good doctor to deal with only the most obviously meritorious cases—women who had been raped, for example.

Women who could pay, for example.

The pricing was exorbitant because they had to limit demand to people they could trust to be discreet. A poor woman, no matter how worthy, could not possibly be served or hear about the availability of Dr. Staley's services because the cat would get out of the bag.

"What happened to the fetuses?"

The Mrs. shrugged. She had no idea. Presumably disposed of with other medical waste.

"What about Dr. Staley's records? Where does he keep them?"

"In his office. His personal terminal."

"What are the passwords?"

She shook her head. "I don't think you can expect me to give you that."

But she was thinking them: *<xanadu. tangent.>*

I thanked her and left.

* * *

We'd been busted before by the security measures in Dr. Staley's office. The question was, did we just go in brazen, or did we tone up the stealth act a bit?

"I don't know what we can do, Jen. He obviously has the place completely wired and microchipped."

"Nothing you can do to disable the surveillance? Nothing at all?"

"Not unless it's centrally controlled. Even then, we'd only be able to suppress the immediate response to our intrusion. There'd still be a digital record of what we did and a photo of who we are floating around in the system."

And there's a kid out there living his last moments of life. Maybe more than one. *What to do?*

"We gotta go in. Tonight. We gotta count on not being able to beat the entire security setup."

"Okay. Here's what that means . . ."

We're back. Didi and I are back, after hours, in Dr. Malcolm Staley's offices. This time we bypass the receptionist's station and go directly to the doctor's personal terminal. Didi slaps a passive read/write on the side of the CPU and gets it to boot up.

<okay, Jen> she says over our private net. *<First password just came up.>*

<xanadu.> I think back at her. The microprocessor at my neck picks up the thought and wisks it into Didi's head.

<second password.>

<tangent.>

<okay. here goes.>

The disk whirs for a long beat, then starts chugging

away as if it's accessing something. I sneak a peak at the screen which says, simply—

WORKING

until the disk drive stutters, then shuts down. We must be in, I'm thinking. I glance back at the screen, only to see—

THIS IS A SECURITY VIOLATION! THIS IS A SECURITY VIOLATION! THE AUTHORITIES HAVE BEEN NOTIFIED AND ALL EXITS TO THE PREMISES SEALED!

Perhaps two seconds later the lights come on. Rent-a-cops hustle into the room, stun wands drawn. Dr. Staley is two steps behind. How'd he get here so quickly?

"Just like you said, Doc." This is one of the rent a cops, the big dumb one. He even has doughnut crumbs sprinkled liberally over his shit brown uniform shirt.

<reboot it, deeds>

<gotcha, boss>

"So, Doc, what did your wife do, 'inadvertently' let bogus passwords slip?"

"We checked on you. We knew you were a capable. She gave you yesterday's passwords. I changed them and put in a trigger to let the whole world know when they were used again, which I figured would be soon."

"And what did you change them to?"

It's a reflex action. People cannot help but think

about the response to a direct question. Dr. Staley is no different. Before he can stop himself he thinks—<*shangri-la, cosine*>—and I push those two words out to Didi over our private net. She enters the passwords, typing faster than the eye can see.

"Dammit! Stop them! Seize the storage device they've got attached to my machine!"

"What's wrong, Doc?"

"She's a goddammed capable, and I just thought of the new passwords. She and her girlfriend are probably on a wireless interconnect. Listen, goddammit, the disk is running! Take them out of here!"

They drag me out, with some minor resistance. They take Didi and the passive storage unit. Dr. Staley looks at me with grim satisfaction as he clicks the ERASE toggle on the side of the unit, wiping out all the data.

Derrick Trent is not at all pleased to see us as potential felons. He is especially not pleased to see us with his bleached blond girlfriend draped all over him like we dragged them out of a warm bed, which, the artless fuck says, we did.

He is also not at all pleased to have to curry favor with his captain to spring Deeds and I, especially not at this hour of the night. But it's either him or I get some high-priced mouthpiece (I'm sure Hollis the insurance man could have helped on this one) to drink coffee with the cops and pal it up for $650 an hour until the wheels of justice inexorably decided to release us, anyway.

"After all this, and this guy, this supposed doc, got all the data?"

Didi looks at me, and I giggle. "That's what he thinks."

"What do you mean, that's what he thinks? I

thought you said he brain-deaded your little gadget right there on the spot."

"Ah, Derrick, he did. But our little gadget was not what it seemed. It wasn't just a storage unit. It was also a transmitter. We took his info and zapped it over our wireless net back to the office machines. When he toggled the switch, the office computer sent Didi back a signal telling her how much data had been received before the goon squad cut us off."

"So," Derrick says, stifling a yawn, "how much did you get?"

"Almost a terrabyte. I'd say about ninety-eight percent of the files."

"Shit. So you girls planned it this way?"

"Sort of. We planned on the phony passwords. We also planned on getting caught. And, Mr. 'I just pulled my tiny thing out of my ugly girlfriend,' we also counted on you getting us square on such a bullshit charge."

"Well, ain't this my lucky day."

"Yeah, ain't that the truth."

We get back to the office after a hard day. Didi begins the laborious task of summarizing the information from Staley's computer. I plop down in my chair in the inner office, wondering what new horrors or wonders Staley's data will shed on the case.

I wonder about the stranger in my dreams.

I wonder about the Zombies that attacked my house. *<judgment is your Truth>*

I wonder where John Doe 4 is.

I must have dozed off, because Didi has to wake me up. The information she has is absolutely nuclear.

"First of all, most of the women Dr. Staley serviced had been raped and were afraid they were pregnant by their rapist."

It makes my skin crawl. Having vicariously experienced rape via the stranger in my head, I know that it goes against "the book" about the crime. Rape isn't about sex and procreation—it's about power.

I hold my breath for a second. I don't like coincidence—no such animal. Edith Wharles, a rapist in my head, a common doc who just happens to perform off-the-books abortions?

I don't think so.

"Did you find Susan Conyers's records?"

"Nope. She goes too far back. Her info is probably off-line somewhere."

"Then I guess I'll just have to ask her."

"Ask her what?"

"The sixty-four-trillion-dollar question."

Susan Conyers waited quietly, smoking a cigarette. I hadn't had the heart to tell her my news over the phone. It had to be in person.

"We had a bit of a breakthrough, Susan."

"Didi said as much on the phone, but wouldn't tell me. You found something, didn't you?"

"Yes, we did. I recognized one of the women in the waiting room. This other woman we also suspect was seeing the good doctor because she wanted an illegal abortion."

I look Susan Conyers in the eye. "This other person, Edith Wharles, was raped and feared she was pregnant by her attacker." Susan says nothing, taking a big hit from her cigarette.

"Look, when I asked you about the father of your children you didn't want to say anything, remember? Yet another dead boy has turned up, but it isn't John Doe 4. That boy may still be alive. So I have to ask the question, don't you see, Susan? I have to ask about the father of your children."

She nods, a stream of smoke ejected from between clenched lips. But she says nothing.

As gently as I can I prod her.

“Susan who’s the father of your children?’

“I told you I wouldn’t talk about that.”

“But it’s important, Susan. Almost every other one of Staley’s patients had been raped. Were you raped, Susan?”

“I don’t want to talk about it. I can’t!”

I’m thinking about Edith Wharles now, wheels spinning in my head. “Were you raped by a man with a serpent’s tattoo on his right arm, just above the wrist on the forearm?”

She’s crying now, sobbing uncontrollably.

“Susan, I’m not trying to hurt you. But you have to help me out here. Did it happen the way I said? Were you raped by a man with a serpent’s tattoo on his forearm?”

She doesn’t answer verbally. But in her mind I can see her response—

<yes>

and her mind’s eye image of the stranger that haunts my dreams, fifteen years younger in her recollection, but the same son of a bitch nonetheless.

Were You Raped?

Mother’s reaction when Susan told her: “Who would want to rape *you*? Are you sure you didn’t encourage this person? Flirt? Dress suggestively? Hmm?”

She was walking home from the pier in Santa Barbara. It was spring, a quiet night, peaceful. Santa Barbara was a well-to-do community and she and Robert lived in a bungalow purchased with Susan’s assets. When

Robert was away "in the field" she liked to take walks at night. Santa Barbara was perfectly safe, unlike LA.

She became conscious of the footsteps behind her, the slight grinding sound of new soles against the concrete sidewalks. She'd risked a glance behind her and seen a white male, six feet plus, dark-haired, slender, muscular, seemingly drifting along the sidewalk fifteen paces behind her. His head was turned toward something across the street, not intently staring at her because, well, because she wasn't pretty. Her friends characterized her as sturdy and dependable. It wasn't strange that this man wasn't looking at her. Men never looked at her.

She kept walking through the central business district, comforted by the people around, even though at 10 PM on a Thursday night it was getting late for folks to be out.

As she cleared the central business district she noticed that the man was still behind her, maybe less than ten paces behind her. And now that the sidewalks weren't quite so populated, he was looking at her. She quietly debated turning and walking back into the central business district and finding a franchise where she could buy a cup of coffee and wait this stranger out.

But it was a nice night for a solitary walk, and the thought that a strange man was actually interested enough in her to follow her was somewhat flattering. It had to be innocent, she thought, because Santa Barbara was the kind of place where it could only be innocent.

She slowed down, thinking that a conversation would establish whether the stranger had any intentions toward her or not. In a moment he was next to her.

"Nice night," she said, looking at him shyly. She hoped her wedding band was prominent on her hand.

He looked her up and down, not saying anything. The street was tree-lined and somewhat dark; the houses were fairly well set back from the sidewalk and the noise from the street. There were no cars about.

He took her arm.

"Excuse me—" she began to protest, but the stranger began to hurt her, half pulling and pushing her along the street. She went to scream and he put his hand over her mouth and shook his head, smiling in a way that made her flesh shrivel.

"Did you enjoy getting fucked by a stranger?"

There was a small park half a block away from where he grabbed her arm. He dragged her; if she couldn't scream she could at least become dead weight. At the entrance to the park he turned to her and pulled her close, one hand groping between her legs. She whimpered, terrified, and he pushed her into the park.

There was a copse of trees that shielded a patch of ground from the houses and the surrounding roads.

"What do you want? Why are you doing this?"

"Get undressed. Get undressed or I will hurt you."

"Please, please, don't do this? Please . . ."

His face held menace as he slapped her, then covered her mouth as she started to cry.

"I'm-not-going-to-tell-you-again," he said slowly. "Get undressed."

She began unbuttoning her blouse as the stranger shucked down his pants. She turned away from his nakedness and gave herself up to her shaking fear that she was going to die.

"Who would want to rape you?"

Yes, who? As he threw her to the ground she saw the serpent's tattoo on his arm.

One last time, she asked, "Why? Why are you doing this?"

And he looked at her as he lay down on top of her, his weight pressing against her pubic bone, and said, simply—

"Redemption."

Sweet Jesus. "Get Derrick Trent on the horn, nowski!"

Didi makes the call; I lie and think it's because of her familiarity with the equipment.

"Detective Derrick Trent," comes over Didi's speaker phone.

"Derrick, it's Jenny. I need you to get the LAPD computer back on-line for the dead boys case."

"Why?"

"Because I suspect there is a genetic link between all the victims."

"Oh, yeah? And who?"

"Each other. I believe they may share a common parent."

"What?"

"Derrick, I don't have time to explain it all now. There's a serial rapist on the loose, and these are his kids."

"Fifteen years worth?"

"At least, yeah."

"Uh, Jen?"

"Yeah."

"Do you know how out of your mind that sounds?"

"It's even better than you think. Each of the mothers had what she thought was an abortion to get rid of the unwanted pregnancy."

"So if they didn't get rid of the baby, someone delivered the kids to the father, who then decides to get rid of them once again, fifteen years later for some reason we can't yet fathom. I repeat my earlier question—do you know how out of your mind this sounds?"

"Run the DNA samples against one another, Derrick. There will be a common link between all the victims. Then tell me you think I'm crazy."

"Who's paying for the computer time?"

"You willing to eat it if I'm right?"

"Yeah, but not if you're wrong-o."

"Fine. I'll guarantee it." I pause for a second, looking at Susan and thinking about John Doe 5. I have a feeling that her other son is still alive and is the boy I've been thinking of as John Doe 4, the boy I saw in JD 3's mind. "Also, Derrick, could you make sure that none of the victims are directly related to John Doe 2?" JD 2 was Susan's "son."

"Directly related? You just said . . ."

"*Both* parents the same."

"Um. Okay. You're paying for this, right?"

"Right."

Derrick clicks off, and my head is reeling. How many possible kids are out there? How many has the stranger killed? Why? Why go through such a bizarre means to have children only to kill them off?

And what to do next? Run an add in the paper?

Hey, if you've been raped, had an abortion by a certain doc whose initials are MS, please call me?

MS—I have to break him. Him and his conniving wifey-poo.

And speaking of first initial "M"s, where the fuck was Mitch?

"Deeds, have you heard from Mitch lately?"

Her head swings back and forth on gimbals. "Nope. But I did finish the research that you wanted on him."

"Yeah, and?"

"You wanted to know why he left the Church of the Resurrection, right?"

"Yeah, and?"

"Well, as late as last week, he's still listed as their prefect and A numbah one son. So maybe he's off working on this Sunday's sermon."

I've asked Didi to pull some of Mitch's writings from the church. But there is something about the bodies that is nagging me, something I should go back to. C'mon, use those private detective skills, girl.

I go back to my diagrams. What else did the bodies have in common besides their daddy?

Of course.

The marks.

Psycogenic purpura. That's what the police reports called them. I need a terminal.

Sitting at my desk, I pull up the files on the dead boys.

John Doe 1 had a mark on his left foot.

John Doe 2 had a mark on his right palm.

John Doe 3 had a mark on his left hand.

John Doe 5 had a mark on his right foot.

Computer, overlay each wound onto a composite body.

WORKING.

Now there was a file in my internal processor about purpura gathered from research sources. In my head I think about a file folder labeled "Purpura" opening and a software agent in my internal accesses the file. If I recall correctly, I only read a part of the file.

I shoot it via my wireless net into the workstation I'm clattering away on.

Access research file "Purpura."

On-screen the composite body showing the wounds on the dead boys shrinks to a window. The display reads:

YOU LEFT A BOOKMARK. BEGIN @ MARK?

Yes.

FILE READS AS FOLLOWS:

See also Stigmata, x-ref purpura.

Stigmata: *Spontaneous flesh wounds that roughly correspond to the injuries Christ suffered on the cross during crucifixion. The stigmatization of St. Francis of Assisi is among the most famous examples, although lay people not associated with the church have been so afflicted.*

St. Francis of Assisi founded a major monastic order and was canonized for his life of incredibly devout faith. Two years before his death during a retreat on Mount Alvernia in Italy he "received" spontaneously the wounds of the crucifixion. His hands and feet had puncture wounds consistent with having been pierced by nails and his side had a wound consistent with being slashed. These wounds appeared spontaneously and were not self-inflicted.

Other spontaneous cases have occurred among persons appearing to be very devout and dedicated to religious worship in general and the worship of Jesus Christ in particular.

Wow, that's really . . . wait a minute. I click on the window composite of the wounds from the dead boys.

Four bodies. Four wounds, one in each hand and each foot.

It can't be. No *way.*

All they need is the wound in the side and marks on the head for the crown of thorns . . .

A tall rapist with a tattoo. Dead boys with wounds that appear to partially replicate crucifixions. Zombies bringing people back to life—resurrection. Where the fuck is Mitch when I need him? Something's wrong there, too. Wait—the street-corner church guy. He seemed to know Mitch.

Keyboard: Computer, find me listings for . . .

What the hell was the name of the church? House of Worship? House of Forgiveness? No. House O' something. Scroll through the listings.

How many fucking flapjack joints could there possibly be in LA? House of Pancakes, House of Pancakes, House of Pancakes, aha! House O' Prayer. Dial.

Ringy ringy.

"Hello?"

"Yes, may I speak with Reverend . . . Cappers, please?"

"This is he."

"Hi. My name is Jenny Sixa. Myself and some acquaintances stopped in your church a few days ago."

"People come to my church all the time. It's what the church is for."

"We were the white people. Two females, and a man whom you recognized as Mitch Belford of the Church of Resurrection."

"Oh, yes. I remember." *Is it me, or did his voice just get icy cold?*

"How did you recognize Mitch Belford, Reverend Cappers?"

"From his speeches."

"Is he a prominent speaker for his church?"

"Are you kidding? Lady, I don't really know why you pal around with him, or why in God's name you brought him to my church."

"I'm uh, lost here, Reverend. What are you trying to say?"

"Have you ever heard Mitch Belford speak?"

"Nope. Can't say that I have."

"He's the most racist man I've ever heard grace the pulpit."

"What?"

"You heard me. He is the most racist person I've ever heard speak."

"I don't understand."

"Read his work. Get ahold of his speeches. Listen to the man's words."

"Are you sure?"

"What, you were thinking this man was some kind of liberal?"

"I . . . don't really know."

"It's all a part of the public record. Look it up and stop wasting my time."

So I do just that.

"Freedom is wasted on those who are unfit to be law-abiding members of society. We have already segregated them in the heart of our cities. But the problems do not abate. We have nibbled at their constitutional rights, but the problems do not abate. We spend millions incarcerating large numbers of them in prisons, but the problems do not abate. We fight wars on drugs, civil wars that pit police against an armed citizenry that we brought into our lives as chattel and expected, suddenly, to become like us. I say listen to the Bible, specifically Leviticus 25:44—'You may acquire male and female slaves from the pagan nations that are around you.' I say that the Bill of Rights is not a God-given right, it is conferred by men and women on like-minded men and women, and it can and should be revoked for those who have proven themselves singularly unworthy . . ."

And there is more, much more. When I think back to that first conversation at my party, it all fits. Mitch Belford had simply edited out the parts of his rap that were utterly racist.

Now the question is, why?

I have Didi pull Mitch's curriculum vitae from the net.

It shows that Mitch Belford spent several years as a "missionary" in the South Central Zone. Even as Los

Angeles County prefect of the church he spent a great deal of time in the zone. In fact, only in the last six months or so have his duties been centered outside of the zone.

Dead boys. Zombies. A stranger in my head. A drug.

And something Mitch said about why he'd "left" the church, about the things he'd heard in confession.

Suddenly I'm willing to bet he can tie some of the pieces of this puzzle together. Uh-huh.

Not wanting to alert the media, I give the ol' Mitcheroo a call. Invite him over. Haven't seen him for a while. Want to discuss old tricks.

While I'm waiting for him to get to the Beverly Hills Hilton I ask Didi to run a backtrace on his number and see if she can find an address. Seems that with all the excitement, ol' Mitchy-boy never told me where he lived. Come to think of it, we always talked on the phone, or met at neutral ground or he came to see me when I needed him. I call Elmo, my party planner, and ask him to pull the record on what address was used for Mitch's invitation to my party. Elmo, the little prick, makes a big thing about how I haven't called him to see how he's doing since the party, like I give a rat's butt, but promises to get back to me with the details. Better yet, I ask him to give the information to Deeds.

In no time, it seems, Mitch appears at my door. He's still got that migrant farmworker look, maybe today's hat is a little different.

"You got here fast." Too fast? Depends on where he lives, Jen.

"I'm sorry I haven't been in touch. It's been hectic."

"Mitch, I came across some interesting information about the case. I thought you might be able to help."

He gets a soda from the minibar and sits in a chair by the window. He gazes out at the smoggy air and says, "Sure, go ahead. Whatever you have, I'm all ears."

So fire away, babycakes. "According to the Church of Resurrection, you never left."

"An error. The church isn't necessarily that cyber-literate or up-to-date," he says, sipping his soda. Not a flinch.

"Really? And I happened to run into that reverend from the street-corner church? You know, the House O' Worship, no, um"—*be convincing, Jenny!*—"House O' Prayer. I was pretty shocked when he said you were the most racist person he'd ever heard in the pulpit."

He turns and looks at me. "You look really lovely today, Jen."

'Scuse me? "Say what?"

"I said, you look really lovely today."

"Hey, Mitch, c'mon now, *focus*. I asked a question. I'm really curious about the answer."

He stretches his legs in the chair. "Y'know, Jenny, I told you this is stuff that I really don't like to talk about."

"Understandable if you're a racist working for a racist faith."

"Don't be ridiculous. Why do you think I left?"

"What's that supposed to mean?"

"I mean that I had an awakening. I couldn't toe the party line anymore."

"But, Mitch, when I think back on what you told that doctor at my party and what you've written, it's almost like what you said at the party was a sanitized version of what you've written. It's as if you cleaned up your act for the party."

He shakes his head and sighs. "Do you also remember that I said that religious organizations had their own internal dynamics and politics?"

"Yeah, vaguely."

"In my former church, you either toed the line or you were excommunicated. Simple as that."

"What about advocating change?"

"Not possible. Not for me."

"Why not?"

He looks me dead in the face and I don't like the sensation. "I made the mistake of confessing to a superior my sins. I had no choice but to go along with the rhetoric."

"You lost me. Confession is supposed to be a sacred trust between you and the person hearing confession."

"What I told my confessor was a secret. Afterward he made it clear, without being explicit, that he would reveal my secret if I didn't go along with things."

"How could he do that without explicitly breaking faith? And how bad could it have been?"

He gives me that look again. "Lifelong celibacy is a gift from God, Jenny. The Church of the Resurrection requires that all its priests be lifelong celibates. When you are ordained you confess to God all your sins, and sex had better not be one of them. As for revealing it, a not-so-subtle hint here or there, all for the purpose of advancing God's works, would have been more than sufficient."

"Are you saying . . . you mean that you and I . . ."

He just looks at me for a long time. Then says—

"I've stayed away for a reason, Jenny. Spending time with you, well, it made me reminisce about things." He gets up from the chair, sets the soda can down on the plush carpet. Stretches.

"Two kids like us, way back when . . ." He shakes his head. He steps toward me.

"It was talking that led us to sleep together, you know. Not romance, not friendship. We talked our way into sex."

"Yeah, so?" I say, but in his head—*<I'd like to talk again. Feel your body again.>*

And I back away. "Look, Mitch, I said before that I didn't think it was a good idea to try to rekindle old flames."

"But I can make you happy. Fulfilled. You're so lonely, Jenny."

"I don't think so, Mitch."

He reaches out to me, caresses the last button on my blouse. Pops it open, revealing a tiny patch of midriff skin. *<I can make you come . . .>*

"Mitch, stop it."

"Jenny, I—it's been so long since . . ."

"Mitch!"

And then the look in his eyes clears. "God, I'm sorry, Jenny. Really. Don't know what came over me."

"Yeah, sure. Occupational hazard. For a woman."

But I look at him closely, then turn away and show him to the door.

And, dammit, I never asked him about stigmatas and the bodies.

He backed away from her hotel. While he didn't have the bandwidth on his wireless network to look at everything his software wizards had culled from her office and her hotel room, he'd been squirted enough bitmaps to get the overall picture.

He had enough of a sense about her to make a move. The terror just beneath the surface of his mind propelled him to do at least that.

Make a move.

The stalking phase was over.

Derrick reaches me at the hotel. "We crabbed a fast processor block and put it on the dead boys' case," he explains.

"And?"

"Computer time's on LAPD. The kids are all linked to a common parent."

"And John Doe 2? Does he have a twin brother in the morgue?"

"Negatory." For Susan I breathe what I think is a sigh of relief. Still time.

"Since we know the mothers are all different, that means Daddy's a killer. And a rapist."

I quickly recount Edith Wharles's and Susan Conyers's stories about being raped, and being pregnant.

"So who are we looking for?"

"Tall man, thin, dark hair, moderately attractive, tattoo of a serpent on his right arm above the wrist, on the forearm."

"Have you thought about getting a composite done?"

"Nope. Not unless Edith Wharles did one when she was raped. You should be able to pull the files from that case directly."

"Gotcha."

And then it's time to play a hunch. "What do you know about the Church of the Resurrection?"

"Isn't that your boy Mitch's outfit?"

"Uh-huh."

"I don't know that much personally. Big friends to the police. Very supportive, always giving money for bigger and better guns and riot control gear."

"Do some digging for me, will you please?"

"On whose budget and with what time?"

"Yours, and, I'm afraid, yours. Bury it where you put the credits for the genetic search."

Derrick rings off.

Sometime later Didi calls me.

"Backtrace on the Mitch phone number. Address is in Santa Monica."

"Can you tell what it is? Apartment? House? Vacant lot?"

"It happens to be the same address Elmo used for your party invite."

"Yeah, and?"

"The party invite was sent to the Church of the Resurrection. The phone listing databases indicate this is their main . . . monastery or something religious like that."

Interesting.

"How quickly can you pull building plans for that place?"

"Depends on how many of the no-show political jobs in the Santa Monica muni government are in the buildings and permits departments."

"Do your best. And do me a favor? Call Susan and tell her that I think her remaining child is still alive."

"Uh, shouldn't you do that kind of stuff, Jenny?"

Jenny, eh? My Deeds is really pushing the envelope of sarcasm here.

"Yeah, I should. But you know how I hate that kind of thing."

"Hmm. I'll see if I can squeeze it in between making coffee."

Whoa. Score one, Didi! I'll have to apologize later.

The next order of business was one Malcolm Staley. I could confront him now that I knew what the basis of his practice was. I link up the vid phone because I wanna see him squirm when I tell him how much I know.

It's about five-thirty in the afternoon when I dial the number. The last patients are probably just clearing out.

As the connection goes through the little screen on the phone fuzzes, then resolves.

But it's not the receptionist I get. Or the good abortionist doc.

"Derrick? What the hell are you doing there?" Derrick Trent does not look happy.

"Homicide, Jenny. Malcolm Staley was murdered about an hour ago."

Homicide. I rush to the office because I need Didi to do something and I think I have to ask her face-to-face. Nicely.

I admit, I'm breathless as I rush through the door. "Deeds! Malcolm Staley was murdered."

Didi just sort of looks at me and continues working at her keyboard. "And?"

Well, doesn't this take the wind outta my sails. "He was murdered at his office," I say as cheerfully as I can. I mean, given that it's murder, right?

"And?"

Cue apology speech on reel one. "Look, Deeds, I know that our partnership sometimes still feels like a bossnership. I know that you are perhaps a bit miffed about continually being ordered/asked to do trivial things. But our partnership, before we became partners, was about inspiration and perspiration. True, perspiration does most of the hard work.

"But without inspiration, there's no direction. Deeds, it worked well before we became partners. It's gotta work now that we are partners. But fundamentally, I think it's gotta work the same inspiration/perspiration way."

"I can solve cases too, you know."

"Yes, Deeds. I know you can."

"And I can do more than make coffee and run errands."

"I know, Deeds. You've already proven that."

Christ, am I talking to the tin man, or what? *If I only had a heart, do-do, dodododo.*

"Staley was popped in his office, huh?"

"Yup. Now you're the one that penetrated their surveillance system, right?"

"Uh-huh."

"You're the one who could hack in and pull the security cam images for the past couple of hours, right?"

"Right again."

"But if you want, we can wait until LAPD stumbles across the fact that there's security cameras in the receptionist area, then fills out a million forms to requisition the images, which by then will probably have been erased from digital storage because they only keep a limited amount of video on hand."

"We could, yes."

"Or, even better, we could wait a few millennia until I figure out how to hack into their systems, right? I'm a bright girl. I'd have the best teacher in the world, right?"

She frowns. "You? The 'clutz who's a putz'? Don't think so."

"Or, you could go in and get what we need. I figure the last couple of hours from his waiting room and the building lobby." *Too bad his private office isn't wired for vid . . .*

"It's gonna cost you, but okay."

Phew.

Man, Didi does the human thing really well. She called up the security people on the phone, made like she was some super bitch from LAPD, and demanded access to their entire system—then had the nerve to tell the poor slob on the other end that if they dumped one picosecond of security images from Staley's building over the next forty-eight hours they'd be up as accessories to murder.

And they bought it. The whole stinky enchilada.

No wonder she has top billing in our firm.

"According to you, the assailant came in, overpowered the receptionist, and went in the back to do herr doctor, right, Jen?"

"That's what Derrick said."

"Okay, this is what I found on the inside of the office."

A man comes in, tall, thin, back to the camera. Shoos the other patient. Jumps on the receptionist, knocks her down, gags her with—

"What is that—a pair of panty hose?" Didi nods.

As he tugs on the inert form of the receptionist he turns toward the camera.

There is a serpent's tattoo on his arm. A slight grin on his face.

My stranger then enters Staley's inner office.

Shit. My mind is reeling. Why is everything interconnected? Why kill the doctor? What does the doctor know that he doesn't want revealed?

How does the stranger know that the doctor has been compromised by me?

You've had that creepy feeling of being watched, Jen.

Surveillance on me?

"What about entering and exiting the lobby? Is there a better camera angle on him there?"

"That's the odd thing, Jen."

"Meaning?"

"He's never in the lobby coming or going."

"So he snuck in. No biggy."

"Perhaps, but look who does enter and exit the lobby right around the time the murder took place." She runs the image file forward.

"Since we're closer to the exit time, I'll show you that first."

She runs the file from the lobby camera.

Oh, my. Have I mentioned my profound hatred of coincidences?

"And when he enters?"

Didi sorts back through the file to the appropriate time.

Yup, I see him. Big as life.

Didi frames the question for me. "What's Mitch Belford doing in Staley's building around the time he's murdered?"

Calm, be calm.

<I can't>

Yes you can.

You are being asked a question.

INITIATE REPLAY Y/N

I can't do it. I can't.

<yes you can. you must>

Well, damn the terror was like a mighty river flowing through his veins, make it stop, make it stop. I don't want to see this.

Press yes. Get it over with.

No.

<no>

Somehow he presses yes—

* * *

He goes into the office, looks at the last remaining patient, tells her to leave. The receptionist looks up, definitely does not like what she sees, not that he isn't decently dressed or something, just the look in his eyes, like his hand was being forced. He knocked her fat ass out of the chair and onto the floor, felt some secret compartment in him open up and came within a few microvolts of neural stimulation of killing her. Panty hose, nice touch, he ties her up, pushes her aside.

It's late in the day, the occupant of the office is engrossed in a journal, taking a break before the last patient, headphones on with classical music blaring. Doesn't hear a thing. He goes into the private office, shuts the door. The doctor looks up from his journal.

"Oh," the doctor says, "it's you." Then he gets angry.

"What in the world are you doing here? Whatever it is, we certainly cannot discuss it now."

He doesn't move. The doctor continues.

"Look. Get out. You want to meet, let me know through the usual channels and we'll meet at one of the safe places."

He takes a step forward. The doctor is still seated.

<bad move> because it gives him leverage. He bears down on the doctor who is no match for his relative youth and strength, and the inner rage comes out in a raging torrent of molten anger like it's burning the tips off his fingers, the pain is so intense that he grabs the doctor's neck, squeezing and twisting, trying to make the burning in his hands/his fingers/his head go away.

<letting it go> yes, letting it go, his arms are made of stone, molten yet hard, strong . . . he twists one way,

then the other, until something lets go, the poor doc is already purple from having his windpipe crushed and now his neck is broken so badly he's practically facing the wrong way.

<letting it go> the sadness and the disgust, letting it all go as he straightens his shirt and gets ready to leave.

REPLAY COMPLETE

(S)AVE/(C)HANGE/(N)EUROBIOLOGICAL REPROGRAM RECORD?

Reprogram, yes, yes, yes . . .

ARCHIVE COPY WILL REMAIN
ENSURE SUBJECT IS ON-LINE. PRESS "ENTER" TO CONTINUE

Yes, yes . . .

and he lays back in the chair and waited until the tiny electromagnetic charges pulsed through the precise portions of his brain.

I suggest that Derrick get a warrant to search the Church of Resurrection.

He, naturally, laughs.

"Based on what? So he was in the building. Big deal. He ain't the guy in the office doing the receptionist."

"Yeah, but you know how I hate coincidence, Derrick. And there's a kid out there getting ready to die. I just know it! They're tieing up all the loose ends, don't you see?"

"What I don't see is how it all interconnects. Loose

ends to what? By whom? And if I don't know, what am I supposed to tell a judge? But, Your Honor, my telepath friend has a really strong feeling about this?"

Damn. There has to be a link. Has to be.

I tell Didi to cue up the security cam files again.

He comes out of it dazed, a headache forming in the front of his head. The display is winking at him and as he moves to answer the question his head begins pounding like the last migraine on earth. It's enough to make him pause for a moment in the chair until his eyes refocus.

And when they do—

1 RECORD(S) ARCHIVED

He doesn't remember archiving any of his memories, but the system is designed to do so automatically just about whenever he has a session in the chair. Is that why he's lying here?

Why he has this awful headache?

He types: *Recall Record.*

The machine's answer:

INITIATE REPLAY? Y/N

and he answers in the affirmative. The machine asks him to ensure that he's fully integrated into the system. Then the replay begins:

"You got here fast."

"I'm sorry I haven't been in touch. It's been hectic."

Lie, lying liar . . .

"Mitch, I came across some interesting information about the case. I thought you might be able to help."

He gets a soda from the minibar and sits in a chair by the window. He gazes out at the smoggy air and *sees his reflection*, then says, "Sure, go ahead. Whatever you have, I'm all ears."

"According to the Church of the Resurrection, you never left."

"An error. The church isn't necessarily that cyber-literate or up-to-date," he says, sipping his soda. *Lying, liar, weird gaps in memories, dates and times missing, lying to cover for it, this loss of self, this sense of having been stripped of layers of himself . . .*

"Really? And I happened to run into that reverend from the street-corner church? You know, the House o' Worship, no, um"—she pauses—"House o' Prayer. I was pretty shocked when he said you were the most racist person he'd ever heard in the pulpit."

He turns and looks at her. "You look really lovely today, Jen." *The truth. Unease/vague/stirring . . .*

She looks incredulous. "Say what?"

"I said, you look really lovely today."

"Hey, Mitch, c'mon now, *focus*. I asked a question. I'm really curious about the answer."

He stretches his legs in the chair. "Y'know, Jenny, I told you this is stuff that I really don't like to talk about." *Unknown. Neither true nor false, made up, possibly true . . .*

"Understandable if you are a racist working for a racist faith."

"Don't be ridiculous. Why do you think I left?"

"What's that supposed to mean?"

"I mean that I had an awakening. I couldn't toe the party line anymore." *Lies . . .*

"But, Mitch, when I think back on what you told that doctor at my party and what you've written, it's almost like what you said at the party was a sanitized version of what you've written. It's as if you cleaned up your act for the party." *Truth? Lost in his own machinations . . .*

He shakes his head and sighs. "Do you also remember that I said that religious organizations had their own internal dynamics and politics?" *Truth. Memory exists . . .*

"Yeah, vaguely."

"In my former church, you either toed the line or you were excommunicated. Simple as that." *Lies??*

"What about advocating change?"

"Not possible. Not for me." *Lies, image of his words stretching thin over a bare wire frame, a design flaw, not enough left to cover the metal . . . sex, sex . . .*

"Why not?"

"I made the mistake of confessing to a superior my sins. I had no choice but to go along with the rhetoric."

"You lost me. Confession is supposed to be a sacred trust between you and the person hearing confession."

"What I told my confessor was a secret. Afterward he made it clear, without being explicit, that he would reveal my secret if I didn't go along with things."

"How could he do that without explicitly breaking faith? And how bad could it have been?"

"Lifelong celibacy is a gift from God, Jenny. The Church of the Resurrection requires that all its priests be lifelong celibates. When you are ordained you confess to God all your sins, and sex had better not be one of them. As for revealing it, a not-so-subtle hint here or there, all for the purpose of advancing God's works, would have been more than sufficient." *sex, sex . . .*

"Are you saying . . . you meant that you and I . . ."

He looks at her for a long second or so, then continues—"I've stayed away for a reason, Jenny. Spending time with you, well, it made me reminisce about things." He gets up from the chair, sets the soda can down on the plush carpet. Stretches.

"Two kids like us, way back when . . ." He shakes his head. He steps toward her. *Sex . . .*

"It was talking that led us to sleep together, you know. Not romance, not friendship. We talked our way into sex." *sex, sex . . . desire . . .*

"Yeah, so?" she says, and he thinks—

<I'd like to talk again. Feel your body again.>

And she backs away. "Look, Mitch, I said before that I didn't think it was a good idea to try to rekindle old flames." *He took her on the ground, the hard dirt, creamy thighs, broken heel . . .*

"But I can make you happy. Fulfilled. You're so lonely, Jenny."

"I don't think so, Mitch."

He reaches out to her, caresses the last button on her blouse. Pops it open, revealing a tiny patch of midriff skin, thinks:

<I can make you come . . .>

"Mitch, stop it."

"Jenny, I—it's been so long since . . ." *sex, sex . . .*

"Mitch!"

And then something goes wrong, and he says, "God, I'm sorry, Jenny. Really. Don't know what came over me."

"Yeah, sure. Occupational hazard. For a woman."

She looks at him closely, then turns away and shows him to the door.

REPLAY COMPLETE

He tears the attachments from his head, frantic because of the replay. *Someone else's memories have leeched into my system!* he thinks frantically. Who is Mitch? Why are his thoughts here?

There was a point in the replay where this Mitch looked out the window and saw himself reflected. It wasn't his face, it was this Mitch person. He runs to the glass walls that enclose the equipment, getting close enough to get his reflection—

No, he sighs. He doesn't look like this Mitch person.

He holds his arm up and studies the reflection of the tattoo. The serpent is angry now, he thinks, but there was no tattoo on this Mitch's arm.

Then who is Mitch? he wonders.

Must be a stranger, he decides.

Keen-eyed private investigator that I am, it doesn't take me long to spot the obvious clue in the security cam footage. I point it out to Didi who actually giggles.

"Can you give me a montage of these two images side by side?"

"Sure."

And I'm thinking about what explains what I'm seeing. An evil but not twin brother?

Inspiration and perspiration. The idea hits me when I go to the bathroom to make sure my mascara is okay.

Christ, if I'm right . . . Out of the bathroom on the run I ask Didi to check something about Mitch Belford for me. It only takes a few minutes of perspiration to get the answers I need.

And the info comes back in the affirmative.

I shoot everything we have over to Derrick and ask him to again to get a search warrant for the Church of the Resurrection and tell him again that maybe if we hurry we can save the last teenager from death as an added beni.

Derrick looks at our stuff.

It doesn't take long.

He agrees.

Now all I have to do is get Susan Conyers here so she can be in on the final chapter of this whole sorry affair. Or so I think.

The next day we gather at the Church of the Resurrection's monastery. Myself, Susan, and, oh, yeah, Derrick Trent and a whole freakin' SWAT team. The place is spooky, medieval-looking, a faux castle with maybe two hundred feet of front lawn and a copse of trees at the edge of the property facing the structure and the front door. We've all parked two blocks away to get ready.

"I thought you said they were police friendly?" I ask Derrick.

"Police sympathetic. Our intelligence says they could be armed to the teeth. This is just a show of superior firepower so they don't get any ideas." And what was it that the reverend from the House O' Prayer said? That the C of R folks came 'round with bodyguards armed to the teeth?

I'll say. Derrick's got his Super Kevlar vest and the meanest-looking weapon I've ever seen him packing.

"Since when are you SWAT-qualified?"

"Hey, one week of special weapons training is mandatory these days. I don't expect to do anything hairy. But I want to be dressed in case there's a party."

Ah, something missing, you say? Well the details are simple.

1. I noticed on the security cam reels that Mitch and the stranger are wearing exactly the same clothes. Coincidence? I think not. When I had Didi split screen the video of my stranger and Mitch Belford, the only difference was the face and the tattoo. Same shirt, same pants, same tacky belt, same shoes, to the extent we could tell.

2. I asked myself whether Mitch had an evil but not twin brother. Then I went to the bathroom to do my makeup. Then it hit me. Morph makeup. Possibly subcutaneous. Programmable. It could certainty account for changing the appearance of Mitch's face, and the appearance and disappearance of the tattoo on his arm. The only question was why?

3. Since we'd busted into so many systems and so many medical provider records searching for the abortion doc, I had Didi do one more extrusion. I wanted to see if Mitch Belford had been the recipient of any plastic surgery, or been a burn victim. The answer came back yes, on both counts. When he was a teen Mitch Belford was badly burned on his face and arm—by his father. There was a criminal record, a newspaper article, and a medical file. Morph makeup was the new rage then, so Mitch has had receptor sites in his skin forever.

These three things combined with the security cam images and our reconstruction of Mitch's last known address were enough for both Derrick and a judge. I can only guess how or why Mitch does the chameleon thing—he must be seriously disturbed.

Susan sits by herself, poor girl, My gut is that John Doe 4 is alive and is her remaining son. I can also only guess at what they've been doing with him . . .

"Derrick, lemme see your weapon." He obliges, grinning like a kid with a new toy.

"It's a combination particle beam/assault rifle. The newest thing in death from long or short range."

"How's it work?"

"A particle beam is just that, a stream of particles at relativistic velocities. Very nasty against soft targets, like tissue, but not so great against shiny or highly polished metallic objects."

"Why's that?"

"You discharge one in a fun house with mirrors, say, and you'll end up with a million holes in you once the beam gets refracted. Or against a shiny metallic object at close range, you'll get what's called blowback as part of the beam gets refracted back at you."

"And the 'assault rifle' part?"

"That's the smaller barrel. Single shot, semi- or fully automatic. High velocity depleted uranium slugs, good stopping power. The bang that will make somebody whimper."

"And the pump action?"

"For the particle beam, the lower, slightly larger barrel. The pump primes the mechanism; it's designed that way to prevent accidental discharge."

Geez, this is nice. "Got any extras?"

Derrick shakes his head. "We got plenty, but I'm not givin' 'em out unless it gets nasty."

"C'mon, Derrick. Have a heart." I like the feel of this thing. It's amazingly light but feels sturdy.

As if to whet my appetite more, Derrick says, "And it's a smart weapon. Plug it into your internal microprocessor and you can get all the status and targeting info right in your head."

"Then you have to get me one."

"Jen, c'mon," he starts, but I point his own weapon at him. "Bang, you are dead because you never learned to play well with others and share."

Finally he relents.

I'm glad, because I have a feeling that things are going to get ugly, quick.

Susan and I are all duded up in Super Kevlar vests and wondering just how dumpy and ugly we look. Derrick comes by and tells us that Susan is going to stay with the vehicles, well away from the skirmish line of police and SWAT baddies, and both Susan and I think:

<bullshit>

"We're gonna send a plainclothes to the front door with the search warrants and try to keep the rest of us out of sight."

"Hiding in the tree line at the edge of the property?"

"Yup."

"Where are you gonna be?"

"In the tree line."

"Then we're with you."

"You I can agree with because you've been in potentially dangerous situations. Her, forget it."

"What if this turns into a hostage situation? She's the only one with a relative inside."

<oh, keyrist!> he thinks. But I look him in the eye, plant a hand on my hip like this is nonnegotiable, and

he relents. I probably cut a meaner figure in Kevlar than I think.

"Hmm. Look, if I agree to this, you keep your head down, okay?" Derrick says to Susan.

We approach the monastery to get ready.

For some reason I'm thinking of the zoners burning down my house as we get close to the place, and the thought makes me absolutely creepy. Gun-happy religious fanatics, eh? Been there, done that.

At least this time I won't be unarmed, I think as I plug the gun's cables into the sockets at the back of my neck and power it up.

<hi i'm ralph, i'll be your gun today>

It whispers in my head. I like this already.

<diagnostics complete. Do you want targeting overlay?>

<not yet>

We settle in well hidden in the tree line. When everyone is in place, Derrick signals the plainclothes who begins walking toward the front door. Derrick hands me a headset so I can listen in on the chatter. In hostile situations with a large number of people it's too confusing to go wireless inside your head. Besides, ralph needs an open line.

"We got any movement on the premises?"

"Negatory. Our guy is about 150 feet from the front door and walking in, over."

"Sharpshooters, anything?"

"Eagle One has nothing here. Roof looks clean."

"Eagle Two has nothing."

"That's a rog. Any of you eagles got a clear shot on whoever opens the door?"

"Eagle One has no joy on that one. My angle sucks; I'd have to go through our guy."

"Eagle Two doesn't have the angle, either, Alpha."

"Okay, I want a sharpshooter set up in the trees right now with a clean flat trajectory at whoever opens the door. If it goes bad, it'll go bad quick."

Hearing this makes me settle into a prone position with the gun pumped and centered on the front door.

<gimme targeting overlay, ralph>

"Where's my third sharpshooter? Our guy is less than a hundred feet from the door."

The targeting overlay is a green haze that comes over my vision as if the visual signal from my optic nerve is being enhanced. The aiming reticule is centered on the doorway and the plainclothes guy is moving toward the door just to the left of my field of fire. I've got a clean shot at whoever opens the door unless the detective moves to the right.

The in-my-head display shows that I'm ready with a particle beam charge, one shot from the fifteen-shot power supply is all I'll have because I'd have to pump the weapon. By the time I do that, the shot and the situation will be over.

"Negative on the third shooter. Nobody's gonna get there in time."

"Damn, okay, fifty feet to go, get ready, everyone. Let's hope it doesn't get nasty."

With each step the detective takes the ground seems to rumble, but I suddenly realize that my heart's pounding.

Forty feet.

Thirty feet.

Twenty feet.

<weapons free, ralph>

and I center the reticule on the doorway. The detective reaches the door. Raises the knocker once, twice.

Waits.

Five seconds. Ten seconds. Fifteen seconds.

A full minute goes by.

"Any signs of movement? All stations check in."

One by one the observers and sharpshooters respond that nothing's moving in the castle.

The detective knocks again. Three times, and hard. Through the tiny parabolic mike under ralph's barrels I get the hollow *thwunk!* of the knocker on the door.

The detective waits, then shrugs, turns away from the door, and holds his hands out away from his sides, as if to say, what now?

And then the door opens.

<steady, steady, gimme low light intensifiers>

but I can see a man in robes flings the door open. He's still in shadow, but I'd recognize the motion anywhere because he's pulling a shotgun level and aiming it right at the detective's back . . .

and I've got the bastard dead to rights, the aiming reticule is a green circle in his center chest, a split second to make a life or death decision.

<take him down>

and my weapon discharges, a flash of smoke in the center of my vision and the parabolic mike picks up what sounds like a thud, and, oh, *yeah,* homeboy has a smokin' hole where his heart used to be, he's falling backward, eyes wide open and seeing nothin', nothin' at all . . .

<vaya con dios, dickhead>

and ralph replies *<excuse me?>*

and then chaos breaks out over the police com band.

* * *

"I've got two suspects with guns on the roof . . ."

"Somebody just broke out the windows on the fourth floor—I can see a weapon . . ."

"Who the hell took down the guy in the doorway?"

"Shots fired, are we clear to engage?"

And gunfire seems to rain from the facade of the building, I see the detective take one in the center of his Kevlar vest—

"You are clear to engage . . ."

"I want an armed patrol to secure the perimeter from any more hostiles, then I want the Go Team in position in ten, copy?"

"Trent, you with the Go Team?"

". . . target has been taken downtown . . ."

". . . downtown . . ."

"Target's down."

And the gunfire trickles away to nothing. Man, that was *quick . . .*

"Go Team in five. Everybody been briefed on the floor plan of this mausoleum?"

"This is Trent. Yeah, I'm going in."

"What about Sid? Anybody gonna scrape him off the front lawn?"

"He's okay. I told him to remain prone until the perimeter is secure."

"Go Team saddle up!"

"Uh, this is Trent. I'm bringing in two civilians."

"What?"

"What? Some idiot got through training without shooting his johnson off and now wants to bring civilians into a hot zone?"

"No problem, he just wants to bring his mommy and his teddy bear."

"Sorry, Jen. I tried and they almost laughed me off the force."

The "Go Team" are the kick-ass boys from the "All Attitude" squad. They go in and clear buildings in hostile situations. Split-second decision making and intimate teamwork are necessary to prevent bad things from happening to the good guys. Five manly men, studly fellows, wolves as Robert Conyers would call them. Derrick is odd man out, the outsider, alone.

I look at him and know that he's worried.

"If anything happens you say the word, Derrick, and wild horses couldn't stop me from going in there."

"Relax, Jen. These guys are professionals." And Derrick sounds like he's trying to convince himself.

The Go Team mounts up and goes in.

"Go Lead, repeat, this is Go Lead, we are entering the premises now. Got one down, looks like a monk, whoa, somebody ruined his day, big fucking hole in his soul . . . okay, place is completely dark, Team, light it up please, hookay, that's better . . . lotta junk and debris, we're in the main hallway, gimme a comeback Alpha control . . ."

"You're loud and clear, Go."

"Lotta debris, like this hallway was barricaded, hold up, Team, we got movement . . . movement in front and footsteps upstairs, you copy, Alpha?"

"I copy, Go. Eagles, look alive. Go Team has possible hostiles on the second floor."

"You there, this is the Los Angeles Police Department executing a search warrant . . ."

I hear gunshots ring out.

"Got some bad attitudes here, boys . . . Alpha, hostiles have opened fire."

"You are clear to engage, Go Team. Eagles one through three, hostile fire reported. You are clear to take down anyone without a friendly IFF tag, copy? Our people are now on the inside . . ."

"Holy smokes! What the hell was that? Alpha, Alpha, this is Go Team, we are under heavy fire from reinforced strong points inside the building in the main corridor, we are pinned, repeat, we are pinned . . ."

The sound of explosions. *"I'm hit! Alpha, I'm hit, they got some heavy-duty stuff in here, estimate fifty percent of my team is down or dead, am requesting an immediate extraction . . ."*

"Roger that, Go Team. Stand by, Eagles five through ten, you are to enter the building immediately and cover Go Team's extraction."

"This is Eagle One. I got what looks like a fire team, second floor, east side of building, two people, possibly a heavy-caliber machine gun . . ."

"Eagle Three. I got a heavy-caliber machine gun, third floor, oh, shit, it just opened up, GODDAMN THEY HAVE MISSILES, TOO . . ."

I see white streaks of missiles contrails coming from various floors on either side of the main entrance like the accusing fingers of an angry god, then red tracer rounds from fifty-caliber heavy machine guns snake from seeming everywhere toward the cops on their way to help Derrick's team. The copse of trees we've been hiding in is being blasted to toothpicks and in the smoke and haze I can see all of Derrick's potential rescuers down and damaged in the grass at least one hundred feet from the entrance.

In two minutes the SWAT contingent is overwhelmed by the pressure of heavy weapons and missiles. The copse of trees is a memory. The LAPD com net is largely silent except for officer down calls and cries for help. Susan and I are cowering behind what's left of a palm tree, which isn't much except a smoking stump.

I check my pistol. Locked and loaded.

I check my rifle. *<weapons free, ralph?>*

And ralph responds in the affirmative. I have fourteen more shots from the energy weapon, and a couple of full clips the heavy conventional ammo.

I don't want to go in there and face certain death. But the gunfire from the castle in front of us makes it clear that the people inside intend to kill everyone on the outside. I look at Susan, who is clearly terrified, and it's infectious, and it makes part of me want to retreat.

And then I remember that I've been there, and when I hear Derrick Trent on the com net:

"Jenny, if you're still out there, I could use some help!" over the sounds of a pitched gun battle my decision is effectively made for me.

I promised him I would come if he called.

"Do you know how to use a gun, Susan?"

"Yeah, my husband taught me some things."

"Find a dead cop and get a pistol and some additional rounds. We gotta go in."

"Are you nuts?"

"You want to find your kid?"

She doesn't answer; bullets sprang off of metal and whiz over our heads.

"Do you or don't you?"

She's frozen.

"No time for a smoke, Susan. In or out? I need you to watch my back."

"Jen! Fuck, it's getting really nasty in here!"

No time. For all my wealth and enhanced immunology, I am not impervious to lead. The roll of the dice. The bitter agony of chance.

I sprint across the lawn, counting the two hundred feet until I'm covered by the building's facade.

Why are these people doing this? Susan wondered as she watched Jenny take off across the lawn. Could it have something to do with her son? Why would her son be here, anyway? What the heck was going on? *But this church is rich. They could get guns. They could get anything they wanted.*

She cringed as a line of tracers came close to stitching Jenny's leg. *She'll never make it by herself,* Susan realized. She grabbed a pistol from a dead cop, then pulled some ammunition clips from the cop's vest.

Oh, like you're gonna save her?

Without really thinking about it, Susan Conyers sprinted across the lawn after Jenny.

If not me, then who?

"Where are you, Derrick?"

"About thirty feet from the open door in the main hall, Jen. I'm about to lose my cover because it's been blasted to shit. I've heard everything from shotguns to Rugers go off from the bad guys."

"How many hostiles are there in front of you?"

"Three, maybe four. But they are well covered, Jen. They've been planning for this."

* * *

I'm in the doorway. I hear movement above me, several pairs of heavy feet, something being dragged. A bullet whizzes over my head.

Get down! and I crouch at the first doorway off the central corridor. There is a monk dead here, holding an assault rifle of some kind. He obviously popped out and started blasting away at Derrick's Go Team before they took him out. I stick ralph's barrel in the open door—

<see any hostiles, fella?>

but there isn't anyone in there. I pass that door, crouch sprint to the next doorway. There's an overturned desk in front of me so I can't see Derrick yet.

Same routine, let the gun's optics scan the room to my right from the doorway. Nothing in there. Clamber over the desk . . .

One of LA's finest is dead on the other side, the front of his head blown out. Must not have checked his six . . .

A section of the ceiling opens up behind me.

Turn and burn. Full auto, depleted uranium shells.

What's left is not pretty.

"Jenny?" Susan is standing at the door to the monastery. The air is thick with blue smoke and cordite; she can smell the blood.

"Yuck." At least she has the pistol ready, squat ugly beetle-looking thing that it is. She has the safety off, knows that she has twenty pulls of the trigger before she has to jam in another clip.

Oh, well. She hears the sputter of a weapon on full automatic.

"Jenny?" she yells and goes toward the sound.

Up on the desk so I can see over the obstacles. There is a wall with gun ports blocking the end of the hallway. It's painted black so that you might not see in the dark until you were right in the kill zone. Into the microphone—

"Derrick? I'm right behind you. I'm going to try to get off a few rounds before I check you out, 'kay?"

"Whatever you're gonna do, do it quick."

I pump the gun, and it cycles with a satisfying *click-clack!* Derrick's crouched behind disintegrating cover and can't bring his weapon into play without getting waxed. So—

<weapons free, ralph>

As I concentrate on the targeting overlay I let the world go green again, careful not to look too closely at the muzzle flashes I see from the fortified wall because those would wash out the optics. I pick out three separate gun ports and points slightly above them. Ralph records my spots. Let's rock.

First spot shows up as an "X" in the display, I put the reticule on the X, and pull the trigger.

Pump the gun.

Pick out the second mark, pull the trigger.

Pump it.

Third mark, fire.

Duck down.

"Derrick? Notice any results?"

Keep going!"

Sighting through the gun's optics, three more gun ports that ralph marks with "X"s.

Click clack!

Fire.

Click-clack!

Fire.

Click-clack!

Fire.

<semi-auto rifle, ralph>

This is where it gets fun. I now pour short bursts through the six holes I just punched through the wall. Oh, man, somebody's screaming.

"Derrick, you hit?"

"Nope. Nice shooting."

"Can you move?"

"Yup. Think so. Cover me."

<particle beam>

Click-clack!

I hear the pitter-patter of Derrick's big cop feet, then movement from beyond the barricade. A lone rifle sticks through one of the gun ports, and I spank his ass with my deadly bright light. The weapon clatters to the floor.

Derrick reaches me, exhausted and covered with dust and blood but otherwise okay.

"So what the hell do we do now?"

"You should go outside and call for backup. I'm going in to find Mitch."

"Jenny?"

Susan walks up, a pistol held limply at her sides.

"I don't know if I can help or not, but at least I'm here."

I know it took real courage for me to walk into this horror show, and I have been through a great deal in my life. I can't imagine what it took for Susan Conyers to come in here.

In for a penny . . .

"Then let's get movin'."

There are people with guns everywhere, Susan realizes as she and Jenny rush downstairs. Didi has apparently fed Jenny a floor plan for this place and from whatever intelligence guides her says that what they are interested in is almost certainly under them.

The staircase is circular, and Susan wonders how much it cost to construct a circular staircase that extends several stories. These religious types must be made of money.

Several times she hears running footsteps and clanging metal doors above them, but the way below seems almost eerily quiet. Is my son down there? Susan asks herself while checking that her gun hasn't suddenly turned to mush in the last thirteen seconds since she last checked it.

Is the boy's father down here as well?

Uh-oh. Footsteps from above, maybe half a flight behind them, coming after her. Jenny the jackrabbit is already almost half a flight ahead of her, and therefore below her. Even if I call out to her whoever's coming will be on top of me before she can get back up here.

Plan A. Stop running and surprise whoever's coming. Kill Them With The Gun. Could she do it? Women like her are sheep. Only men are kill-or-be-killers. Wolves.

Rapists.

A shot *spang-g-gs* against the metal staircase right near her foot. The abstract notions of guns and bullets vanish. This is the real deal.

Stop running.

Breathing hard, listening to the footsteps quickening down toward her. To the footsteps, and her own heart, its rhythm labored, her chest heaving. Raise the weapon to the point where she would see her pursuer curling toward her on the stairs. Apply some pressure to the trigger to get ready.

She saw the tattoo first, her eyes drawn to it as if by magic, and then the face that she'd reviled and loathed for fifteen years. Part of her wanted to pull the trigger to kill this maggot, part of her curled up in fear. She hesitated.

So the stranger hit her over the head, scooped her up, and carried her up the staircase.

The running helps me clear my head. Down the steps, with Susan behind me, I begin to have second thoughts about the wisdom of what we're doing. After all, John Doe 4 was forsaken by his mother and was destined to be no more than biomedical waste. Not that Susan can be blamed for her decision, it's just that John Doe's existence creates a set of problems that simply should not exist. Does Susan get to exert parental rights that she voluntarily relinquished? Does John Doe 4 have to live as her son given the overwhelming evidence that Susan doesn't have children (she had an abortion, remember?).

Wait. I stop running. There is silence within twenty or thirty feet that shouldn't be there. Susan isn't that far behind me, so where are her footsteps? Where is she?

I open myself up for her thoughts and get nothing. Close my eyes, listen to the voices in my head, and I get nothing.

Something's wrong.

He carried her off the stairwell, making sure that no one would see him carrying a woman. It was important to keep the outsiders from the lower levels and they were perilously close to his machines now. Too close. He had no clue who the woman was, only that she'd pointed a gun at him as her emotions played out over her face. At one time he may have been her rapist, but specific memories like that had long since been expunged by his guilt and his equipment.

Besides, at this point, he didn't really matter anymore.

There is a corridor door set flush into the stone walls of the stairwell, hidden as we raced past it on the way down but now carelessly left open. The corridor is dark, which engenders all kinds of feelings of caution and fear. I hear no other footsteps on the stairs, only the distant shouts and occasional thumps of heavy shells and missiles pounding the outside facade of the castle as Derrick's reinforcements begin reducing the aboveground structure to rubble. I hear no thoughts from nearby, so clearly this way will lead me to Susan.

<see anything, ralph?> I ask my companion as I point down the corridor. The green wash of his enhanced optics take over my visual field, always with the green aiming reticule in the center of the vision.

Susan's brain stuttered back on-line because of an utter sense of fear. The stranger was taking her someplace so he could rape her again! Her eyes snapped open. Her gun was gone, probably taken by him. All she had was her fists.

She'd begged him not to assault her.

She'd asked him why, why?

She slapped him in his face as hard as she could, hard enough so that he dropped her.

As she was looking at him, his face changed, the tattoo disappeared, and he became Mitch Belford.

Now that, she thought, *was creepy.*

I heard Susan's surprised scream and ran toward the sound. There was a second corridor at right angles to the first and I saw the two of them, Susan, and what looked like Mitch, at the far end. I ran as fast as I could, ignoring the doors leading off the corridor and the possibility that someone with a gun might appear in response to Susan's screams.

"Susan! It's Jenny!" I yelled as loud as I could, but Mitch was running, leaving Susan in his wake. I aimed my rifle down the corridor—

<how far to the end of it, ralph>

<range=85 meters>

and squeezed off a rifle shot just to keep him running. I reached Susan in short order.

"Are you okay?"

She nodded. "That was the weirdest thing I've ever seen."

"What was?"

" 'Slap-me-I'm-Mitch.' I wonder what tangled psychological baggage is behind that."

"C'mon, let's go find out."

I don't stop to listen to her objections, I just haul her to her feet and drag her along with me.

The corridor dead-ends into a T intersection. Mitch ran left into a section of hallway that runs downhill. Susan and I hustle to try to keep him in sight, and the best I can do is catch a glimpse of his back as he runs.

We're in a tunnel now, somewhere beneath the foundation. The walls are rough stone with lights strung every fifteen feet or so, the floor is smooth hard white tile. Our feet pound as we chase him. I get the strong sense that answers to the bizarre mystery are just up ahead of us.

Then to our right the wall opens up on a cavern festooned with candles and a plain heavy wooden table.

The candles are cold and stubby, frosted with wax residue from the last time they were used, and I get a vision from John Doe 3's memories of this same place with the candles lit, and John Doe 4 being dragged away up this tunnel toward a glassed-in room . . .

. . . which is in front of us. Two rooms, one festooned with computers and a couch. The other glass is opaque. Mitch has sealed himself in the equipment room and seems strangely comforted by the mere presence of all that equipment . . .

<weps free, rifle, ralph>

I think, because I'm gonna shoot my way in if I have to.

Mitch/the stranger is standing in the computer room. He seems lost.

I pound on the glass.

"Where's the kid?" I yell. He looks at me, then apparently turns on the external speaker.

"I . . . in a special place." His voice booms out into the tunnel.

"Why did you want these kids?"

"They weren't wanted by their parents. They were pure. Immaculate."

"But you raped and inseminated the mothers."

"I'm a priest. I have absolved myself of sin."

Susan: "How the hell could you do that?"

He barely glances at her. "These machines, this equipment. It manipulates memory. I absolved myself of my sins by erasing my memories of what I did."

"But you remember! You remember her!"

"I know only about the project. The details I have erased. I know that I committed grievous sins, but the project demanded it."

"You mean the kids?"

"Yes."

"Why did you need immaculate children?"

"Immaculately conceived children. Once the fetuses had been 'aborted' they were, in effect, resurrected by us, here."

"Why?" Susan cries, but I'm way ahead of her.

If you can manipulate memories, you can influence personality. If you can influence personality from birth, you can create a personality from a template of memories and experiences downloaded into the brain.

The stigmata . . . the Church of the ***Resurrection*** *. . .*

I splinter the door frame with the butt of my rifle. Give it one more good crack and the wood shreds around the lock and we're inside, facing him. He stands there, seemingly ready to die.

"I'm going to ask you once. Where is the last boy?"

"I'm not going to tell you that. We've worked too hard and sacrificed too much. Besides, the process is pretty much complete."

I pull the trigger once, single shot, and a single high-velocity slug blows out his left kneecap. He goes down in a yelp of incredible pain; and I think: *<good for you, motherfucker>*

And say again to him, "Where's the last boy?" I walk up and place the hot barrel of the assault rifle against his forehead and it sizzles just a touch as it burns a nice round little "O" in his skin.

"I," he starts through clinched teeth, "won't tell you. Kill me it you want . . ."

I shove the hot barrel in his mouth. "Don't fucking tempt me, asshole."

He shakes his head.

<weps free particle beam, ralph>

Click-clack! I rack the gun. Point it at his crotch.

"This is a particle beam. In about ten seconds your cock will take a ride to agonyville at relativistic velocities. Where's the kid?"

"You can't get to him now. You're too late!"

"Where the fuck is he?" My finger twitches a little on the trigger.

"Go ahead. Do it!"

I haul the weapon away from his privates, aim it at a computer terminal, and fire. Poof! From where he's lying he can see the gaping hole in the monitor that wasn't there a sec ago.

I smile at him. *Click-clack!* Rack the weapon.

Point it at his dick.

"Watch my trigger finger. Now where is the kid?" Real low and menacing, I take all the slack out of the trigger and then some, and his eyes go wide.

"Next door."

We get the lights on and the glass clear even without the benefit of the computer monitor. John Doe 4 is strapped to an apparatus much like the couch in this room except that he's suspended upright against a wall. He is wearing a headset of some kind that is reminiscent of the images I took from JD 3's mind. His arms are outstretched and his legs are spread slightly. He is not wearing shoes.

Suspended over his outstretched arms are vials of yellowish liquid.

Zombie.

"How long has he been in there, and how do I get him out?"

"You can't get him out. The room is sealed. The glass is shatterproof and would stop a tank shell. He's in the final stages of the program."

I tell ralph to go full auto on the assault rifle. I aim at the glass far enough away from John Doe 4 so he won't be injured by the flying shards.

I pull the trigger. Full auto.

Rock and roll.

It's a long burst of sparks flying, then hot lead (or should I say depleted uranium) bouncing around the room as the glass punches back my mere bullets. *Ricochet is a bitch . . .* within seconds so many fractured shells are whizzing around that I get bitten on the back of my leg by one, then several seem to attack me all at once. I go down, releasing my finger from the trigger bleeding and cut in half a dozen places, incredulous that the glass hasn't even cracked.

Susan looks okay, just a scratch, but I'm now lying in a pool of blood, Christ looks like a major artery, and I'm feeling myself to see if I can figure out where the bleeding is coming from.

"Susan, help me! I'm bleeding like a pig and I can't find the wound!"

She gets up calmly.

"You can't find the wound because it's not you bleeding."

"Then who?"

It's a stupid question. I look at Mitch.

He took a slug in the meaty part of his right thigh. His femoral artery is toast, and I can tell from the sickly look on his face that he's bleeding to death. Quickly.

I crawl to him. "You fucking bastard. You can't die like this. Not now! Tell me what you intend to do with this kid!" *<what is the Truth?>*

He looks at me, his pulse fading, his life signs diminishing right before my eyes. I catch one thought, then another more chilling notion of fear underneath it all, fear that connects with something hidden away inside me, *something old mother told me without telling me . . .*

<tell your boyfriend . . .>

Mitch confirms my suspicions. You see, the *Church of the Resurrection* isn't trying to bring back the Three Stooges. *<. . . this is your Truth>*

Susan and I look through the glass to the next room. John Doe 4's eyes are closed, and as we watch, a slash wound appears on his abdomen, all by itself . . .

John Doe 4's thoughts were swirling. Pontius Pilate paced slowly, then asked him again.

"Art thou King of the Jews?"

"If I am, shall I offer proof to one such as you?"

"A statement would suffice."

"A statement would establish guilt."

"So I ask again, art thou King of the Jews?"

"And I say again, is the truth what ye seek? Or the establishment of guilt?"

Pilate, exasperated, left the room and addressed the throngs awaiting his judgment on this Jesus of Nazareth.

"I can find no guilt in this man. He does not admit his crimes, nor does he blaspheme."

There is a murmur, and one of the crowd asks for Barabbas. Barabbas comes forward and accompanies Pilate into his residence. He looks at Jesus of Nazareth, pulls a blade from his robes, and cuts him deeply . . .

Susan and I are desperate to get into the room and release the young man. I pick my rifle up, noting that it seems heavier now, and that my wounds are bleeding more intently with each movement of my aching muscles. Maybe I can use the particle beam to punch a hole in the glass . . .

<weps free, particle beam, ralph>

and note the green counter in the lower left-hand corner of my gun vision shows that I have five shots of the energy weapon left.

But it's glass that I'm shooting at, with a beam weapon. Will it just go through the glass? Or will it punch a hole in it?

Worse, the room with JD 4 is full of equipment and stainless steel. If the beam goes through and hits the shiny metal, it could reflect and kill all of us or JD 4 in an instant.

Do I chance it? Getting dizzy. Maybe I can bang down the door instead . . .

But the door is glass framed by stainless steel, not wood. The hinges look reinforced. Even the lock is a heavy-duty brass number with a numeric keypad for entry . . .

. . . he was brought out of Pilate's residence scourged and crowned with thorns. The crowd, the angry crowd, is as one as they cry out for his crucifixion. Pilate hesitates, then tells the crowd that the punishment is for them to decide, but the hew and cry of their blood lust cannot overlook that they cannot do so legally.

"He claims he is Jesus, the son of God!" one of them yells, and Pilate again hesitates, afraid of judging this stranger.

"Kill him if you wish to court favor with Caesar!" another of them cries. Pilate relents, and does not look Jesus of Nazareth in the eye as he takes his place in his court; Jesus is brought before him to be judged.

And he says to the crowd, "Behold your king . . ." and the crowd screams for blood, screams for crucifixion.

And Pilate says, "So judged, I deliver Jesus of Nazareth unto you . . ." and he is taken away . . .

"Stand back, Susan." I aim the particle beam at the lock on the door. I don't want to risk shooting bullets and having them fly back in my face again.

<warning! target is not suitable for energy discharge!> ralph whispers in my head. I tighten my finger on the trigger.

<warning! blowback potential is high, prospects for injury exceed safe discharge confidence limits!>

So I close my eyes, and pull the trigger.

And scream, "Y-a-a-a-a-a-a-ahhhhh!"

. . . and he screamed as they hammered the first nail into his hand, as they affixed him to the crude wooden cross, he screamed in his mind over the pain . . .

The lock is damaged, but not enough. My face and hands feel like they've been severely sunburned by the blowback from the particle beam and I'm leaking blood out of what feels like a million wounds. I'm so fucking tired. And I look at John Doe 4, and see that another stigmata has appeared, in his right palm.

You have to hurry, Jenny.

Click-clack! I rack the weapon. Point it at the shiny brass lock on the door.

Close my eyes.

Pull the trigger . . .

"Ya-a-a-a-a-hhhhh!"

* * *

He convulsed a bit as they moved to his other hand, as if he could already feel the impact of the coarse wooden mallet on the nail, as if his flesh had already absorbed the impact, as if the mallet had already swung down to drive the nail into his hand . . .

Holy smokes. There are black flakes on my hand that used to be parts of my skin. I look inside the room, where the third stigmata, this time on John Doe 4's left palm, has appeared. The lock is damaged, but not nearly ready to give.

I rack the weapon. *Click-clack!*

Aim it at the lock.

Close my eyes.

Ya-a-a-a-a-a-ahhhh . . .

The pain was beginning to make him delirious. They moved to his right foot. Took careful aim with the mallet poised over the nail . . . he watched in morbid curiosity as the mallet swung down driving the nail through his flesh and through the bones in his foot . . .

I rub my face because it itches, and more tiny black flakes of skin come off in my hand. The lock is damaged now, and I put my bruised and bleeding shoulder to the door to force it open, but it only rattles and does not give.

John Doe's right foot has been stigmatized with the wounds.

You are running out of time, Jen.

I don't have the strength to pump the weapon.

John Doe convulses on his stainless-steel cross.

Damn it, bitch, pump the weapon!

<i can't>

Pump it!

Clack-clack!

Point. Pull the trigger.

Scream, *but screaming is pointless . . .*

. . . his left foot now. They drove the nail through his left foot and pulled the wooden cross upright for the world to see Jesus the son of God nailed to his cross. Time blurred as the computer-induced pain sapped his vitality, as the program sped through the hours until it was time for him to die.

Large patches of burnt and blackened skin are falling off my hands and face. The lock hasn't let go, not yet, and I don't dare risk a glance at Susan because my doubts about this whole endeavor will bring me literally to my knees. Is this the good fight, to prevent the reincarnation of a two-thousand-year-old myth? To deny the resurrection of God and assert the rights of a woman who has forsaken this child born of agony?

The last stigmata appears on his left foot. He stirs, moaning, his mouth open in pain, and I can see the effects of the ordeal rippling through his body in much much faster than real time . . .

I have to break the lock open. *One shot left.*

Oh, shit. I have to pump the weapon. I can barely stand up.

<go on, jenny, pump it>

and I try, I swear I try, but there's nothing left . . .

Pump it!

. . . nothing . . .

PUMP IT!

<I can't>

And some sort of alarm goes off in the next room,

and I can see that a computer has been monitoring John Doe 4's vital signs, and I can see that the signals are inexorably going flat—the boy is dying, the computer is inducing his death much much faster than real time, but of course, they didn't need to conform to some sort of convention concerning His Death, they could have made it up as they went along . . . *you don't have time for this, Jenny . . .*

Pump it, you stupid bitch!

<i just fucking can't>

PUMP IT, DAMN YOU!

<no . . . can . . . do!>

HE'S DYING IN THERE! PUMP IT!

Click-clack!

Pull the fucking trigger.

But I forget to close my eyes, and the hard white flash is more than enough to blind me.

He died in agony, the pain of his wounds tormenting him until he lost consciousness, and they left his dying body on the cross to whither. And he heard a voice.

<it is time for you to return>

whether it was an instant or a millennium after his soul departed his flesh he could not say.

Susan Conyers put all her strength into a last heave at the door. Jenny was down, her face and hands burned black, her eyes unseeing. Jenny had gotten her this far, and it was up to her to do the rest. She blasted her shoulder against the door, hoping the lock would give. It was feeble enough, shorting and smoking from the abuse that Jenny'd administered with that awful gun of hers. But it did not give.

She looked at her son, watched in growing alarm as something in the apparatus he was in buzzed, and the yellow liquid vials suspended above his arms began emptying into the intravenous tubes that ran into her lost son's arms. She didn't know about Zombie, Jenny had spoken about it in hushed whispers to Didi and the others, but never to her.

They're poisoning my baby, she thought, and smashed the door open with one last desperate collision.

The spots in my eyes clear quickly enough for me to see the door smashed open and Susan Conyers climbing up onto the rig that contains her son, formerly known as John Doe 4. I notice that the Zombie has already been pumped into his veins, but his displays, from what I can tell, are still flat-lined. I should go in and help her try to revive the boy, but I cannot for the life of me move a single millimeter from where I am.

And then the damnedest thing. There is a little crackle of electricity, and Susan yelps, and the boy's readouts begin to climb, heart rate and pulse coming back, breathing, neurological activity. Moreover, there is this weird glow around the boy that I'm sure isn't the result of any equipment, a pure white halo of light that makes his skin seem translucent, as if he could fly away if he wanted to.

And then, most of all, Susan climbs the apparatus and looks into his eyes as they open, the look on her face so tender and gentle and full of wonder, the touch of their hands all the more incredible because it should never have happened, it simply should never have happened . . .

* * *

He awoke from the dead unsure of what to expect from his surroundings, swaddled in the certainty that he was the son of God reincarnated, hallelujah. Fifteen years of programming had twisted his story and history to suit this peculiar set of facts, so it did not seem unusual for him to be strapped into some odd-looking device awaiting an acolyte to free him.

But his programming was still vulnerable, his fix on himself still fluid. He'd been programmed with extraordinary belief that wasn't quite innate yet. The first few seconds after awakening were therefore thought to be key.

And the first person that he saw, that he touched, was a woman.

And he asked her . . .

"Who art thou?" as Susan took his hand and kissed each one of his fingers.

And she replied, "I'm your mother."

The warmth from her son's eyes was unlike anything she'd ever seen.

"Mary?" he asked her. Susan smiled, and then shook her head and replied . . .

"No, Susan." And she didn't look like his mother, and of course his mother's name was Mary.

Or was it?

And I saw Susan Conyers touch the boy's hand, murmur something to him, listen, and then murmur something back.

The boy looked profoundly puzzled. And Susan spoke some more.

And the halo around them vanished.

EPILOGUE—SOUTH CENTRO

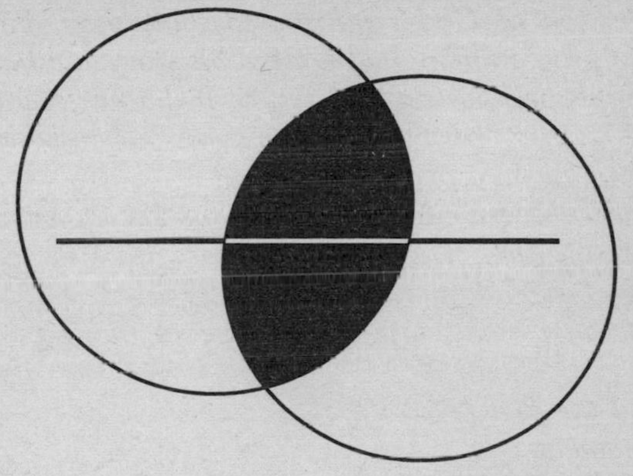

Christmas Day, 2053

When you accept the state of being a stranger, you are no longer a stranger. I have been an exile when everything around me seemed strange and everybody was a stranger. Once I accepted that I didn't have to belong and I didn't have to be part of the world, then I was free to be part of it. There was a paradoxical release of the spirit. The world became mine when I was no longer holding on to it.

—Satish Kumar

I spend days now, wandering South Centro, listening for echos of old mother, looking for the legacy of our encounter. Today is a hot sunny day, the smog not so bad, the crowds preoccupied with the hard scrabble of life with no money on the ultimate consumerist holiday of the year. The landscape is all the more bleak because it is devoid of the signs of Christmas; in the zone this day is like everything else in western society—*meant for other people*. And that is a portion of the Truth that I so desperately seek.

Poor Mitch. He told me many things as he lay dying, as I asked him, *<what is the Truth>* and he thought *<abomination>* and I thought, who did you love, Mitch? Who could have helped you?

Not I, said the fox. Not I, said the hen. And I wonder, did you hate us all, Mitch? Your mother, your father, me, all the women . . .

. . . all the women . . . Mitch, who did you love?

Certainly not me. When I lay with Mitch so many years ago I felt something, we both did. Whether it was passion or telepathy, something happened between us that was both wondrous and scary. A switch opened between us, not like the other time, a connection so powerful that I thought to myself, aha, now I'm at the height of my power as a woman, now I am connected to my lover and no longer estranged from the world. But Mitch had turned away, his passion was something separate and apart from me; I looked up and realized that Mitch had left me, that he had left the building and I was just another—

<who did you love?>

—*door*. But that proto-telepathic link stayed with him, poor Mitch, as if that moment of connection was something that he could give people like a gift and his refusal to look at me after like he'd found a secret that he wanted to share with a whole world of women. No phone calls, no responses, running away to be a priest with a terrible proud secret

<i can make you come>

Oh, God, Mitch, why are men such fools? He got this taste from me, of something that he could never duplicate, not in a hundred years of secretive procreations, not in a thousand dalliances with women, not even with those he forced in frustration, not even as he cried out to me through that something we once had. Goddamn you, Mitch! why did it have to be you, why did it have to be that way, Zombie and the brutal reality of guilt unrequited by your stupid faith? Why did he twist away from me and turn to his God with whom he could not lie? Jesus never said

<i can make you come>

and never could have condoned the lust for power from the little boy whose mother had betrayed him and father denied him, denied his very humanity, the power over women, man's power that he tried so desperately to make bow down to God. Consumed with faith, isn't that what he said, wasn't that the reason why he left me alone to the vagaries of my own troubles?

He was supposed to be a man of faith, a man of God, so much power . . .

<i want to touch you again>

Faith—*thou shalt not fuck*—faith in a church full of celibates, faith in the face of discreet homosexual dalliances, *faith that he liked women*, faith that he could resist, *that he didn't need me, didn't love me at all*—faith, his only shield against his sick needs, his only shield against me, all-consuming faith—

And then he met old mother.

Poor me. I touched old mother here in the zone, the feel of death in her mind, the feel so intense that I blacked out . . .

. . . because it was like the end of nowhere, inside the event horizon of a black hole, everything fucking fading away, fading . . . time and eternity meeting inside the hollow core of a precious second, life an infinite river of hollows wasted forever because it is gone, fading, fading, the pressure of transition intense as it loses significance, as you lose significance, as life loses, as substance loses, as love and hate and emotion loses form, fading fading, *gone*. Mitch was headed in the same direction, last I saw. Good luck, asshole. I hope your faith includes some notion of what kind of hell awaits you. For what you did . . .

Mitch needed boys that they could program into gods. Frantically needed them, and just to get the five finalists he had to attempt to propagate hundreds of times. And of the five, all came close, all believed, all manifested a portion of the stigmata, but Susan's second son, he was the one, the true believer. And part of me wanted to believe, too, part of me wanted to deny what I knew, part of me is afraid of the terrible secret in Mitch's mind, the one he learned here, in South Centro, the one passed to me as he lay in a pool of blood, *fading, fading* . . .

Old mother is awake. Her resurrection was necessary because her work is unfinished. The destruction and the rage of South Centro hides something special, something Mitch stumbled upon during his missionary work here early in his career as a priest.

And if not artificially re-created by us, where is God? Old mother explained it to me herself, *the messiah is here, somewhere, here in South Centro*. A teenaged boy with dark skin, living in the valley under the shadow of death . . . living in a society where basic rights and dignity are meant for other people. The messiah, here.

And Mitch knew this to be true.

And so I walk, searching not for redemption but for self, for the hope that I've done the right thing. The notion of God emerging from this wasteland is not comforting, not some *voodoo chile* of a conjurer like old mother, not some *brother* singing amen. This is a stranger that I fear

<the fear of the lord is the beginning of wisdom>

because old mother shared her vision, not of a second coming, but of a second . . . crucifixion. This was Mitch's darkest fear, why he wanted to prevent the emergence of the messiah here, because he knew there will be people who cannot accept a black man as their lord God and savior—

That this time there will be no cross with nails—

That they will burn this *nigger* god in a *nigger* church, this time.

And the Truth, the passwords to heaven, will be lost, lost in flames sprouting from old mother's eyes, lost in the death of a second son, lost forever in cruelty.

Judgment. On Christmas evening it happens that I am standing in a crowd in the South Centro Zone, near an old building getting jostled by people moving aimlessly past. Music pours from the tenement, laughter and loud voices. Music, and then . . . the sound . . . of helicopters, perhaps three, and the crowd disperses and I stand there for a moment and wonder why.

The gunships clamp down on the roof of the tenement and the music stops, shouts from inside, action dimly perceived through an open hole in the facade where a window used to be. Suddenly I am standing alone except for a young black man, perhaps sixteen or so, and his grandmother, both of whom are looking at me intently. And then there is a sound of wood splintering, LAPD kickin' 'em down, shouts of "Police!" and the boy turns toward the window just as the SWAT team lets go with a barrage of shells, full metal jackets backlit by the muzzle flash of weapons on full automatic, the glitter of the rounds in stark neon contrast to the damage they cause the flesh. And people die in the shadows of their screams, cut to pieces as the young man and I watch, cut to ribbons as we watch the machine guns strobe the life from a room full of people.

And old mother looks at me, a gentle hand on the boy's shoulder and thinks

<this is your Truth>

as the screams die under the impact of heavy shells—old mother nods to the teenager—

<this is your God>

and I think not of the crime or the punishment, not of the cops and their duty, nor of the victims and their families.

<created in this image>

but of the nature of our cruelty, of a young messiah living in the valley of the zone under the shadow of death, knowing too well all evil wrapped up in the things meant for others . . .

<judgment>

I wake screaming from dreaming of old people gambling, playing baccarat while they die, the perfect glitter of the casino in stark neon contrast to the corruption of their flesh. I wake sweating knowing that my image of purgatory is that of a benign God, these things meant for us.

<how can we know of His existence and not be healed>

A benign God, but no less cruel . . .

<how can I know the passwords to heaven and never be told what they mean>
than we are.

Eventually I go back to sleep in glittering isolation, gambling that tomorrow will be a better day. I lay my head down, clutching at the strands of a life whose importance I have yet to fathom, surrounded by baubles I have yet to disavow, alone but for the old people who haunt my dreams, alone,

hoping to fill the void in my heart with faith,
because the only thing that resides there now
is desperation.

ABOUT THE AUTHOR

Eric James Fullilove is a CPA, an MIT graduate, and a former finance manager at CBS. He was also chief operating officer of a not-for-profit corporation that provides housing and services for homeless persons with HIV and AIDS. He lives in New Jersey where he is at work on his next novel.